"God can heal <...> you know," Ellie told Asher gently.

"Yes, of course, but—"

"But you must allow Him to do it. You must be willing. Because He surely has some lucky woman picked out for you."

Asher lifted his eyebrows. "Oh, really?"

Ellie nodded. "She'll admire all your sterling qualities."

"What exactly is a sterling quality?"

"Well, in your case, confidence, kindness, intelligence. Plus, you obviously value family. And, of course, you're handsome."

"Handsome," he repeated.

Then she ducked her head and confessed, "You have gorgeous eyes."

His world tilted, leaving him clinging to the very edge of reason. What on earth was going on? He couldn't be attracted to Ellie Monroe. She was too impulsive, too talkative, too...everything!

Especially too pretty.

From now on, he would be on his guard—stern, disciplined, wise—just as a man in his position ought to be.

But something told him that being on his guard might not be enough to combat the charms of Ellie Monroe.

Books by Arlene James

Love Inspired

ARLENE JAMES

says, "Camp meetings, mission work and church attendance permeate my Oklahoma childhood memories. It was a golden time, which sustains me yet. However, only as a young widowed mother did I truly begin growing in my personal relationship with the Lord. Through adversity, He has blessed me in countless ways, one of which is a second marriage so loving and romantic it still feels like courtship!"

The author of more than seventy novels, Arlene James now resides outside Dallas, Texas, with her beloved husband. Her need to write is greater than ever, a fact that frankly amazes her, as she's been at it since the eighth grade. She loves to hear from readers, and can be reached via her website at www.arlenejames.com.

An Unlikely Match
Arlene James

Love Inspired

Recycling programs
for this product may
not exist in your area.

LOVE INSPIRED BOOKS

ISBN-13: 978-0-373-81545-6

AN UNLIKELY MATCH

www.LoveInspiredBooks.com

Printed in U.S.A.

You have granted him the desire of his heart and
have not withheld the request of his lips.
—*Psalms* 21:2

For Faith Itai Manase, adventuress, world traveler, nurse, friend, daughter of my heart.
I am so proud of you!
Love always,
DAR

Chapter One

Attorney Asher Chatam recognized a summons when he received one, though he could not imagine what legal advice his aunties needed so urgently that it would require his immediate presence. He shrugged out of his camel hair overcoat and surveyed the front parlor of Chatam House, the antebellum mansion where Chatams had resided for generations, including his maiden aunts, triplets in their seventies who had lived in the great house for their entire lives.

As always, Odelia first captured the eye. Wearing royal blue, she had anchored a crown of matching feathers in her fluffy white hair. Speckled, light blue beads the size of robin's eggs dangled by golden chains from her earlobes, completing the theme of her costume. Hypatia, her sister's polar opposite, in expensive bronze silk and a neat silver chignon, placed her delicate Limoges teacup on its matching saucer and graced him with a smile from her customary wingback chair. Meanwhile, Magnolia—known to her many nieces and nephews as Aunt Mags— garbed in her usual frumpy cardigan and shirt- waist dress, her iron-gray braid hanging over one shoulder, beamed her frank enjoyment of his sur- prise at the room's occupants.

Kent Monroe, a pharmacist well past the usual age of retirement, was Odelia's erstwhile fiancé from at least half a century ago. A barrel chest had long since given way to a serious paunch, now bisected by gray suspenders and shielded with a pale blue shirt, topped with a jaunty red bow tie that sat atop his jugular like a strangled cherry crowning a generous scoop of blueberry ice cream. After his failed romance with Odelia, it was generally assumed that Kent Monroe would forever keep a cordial, mannerly distance. And he most likely would have, in the normal course of events. But the normal course of events had been greatly altered.

Asher narrowed his eyes suspiciously at his baby sister. At twenty-three, a full fifteen years his junior, Dallas was as impulsive as her short, frothy hair was red. An inveterate romantic, she had sighed over Odelia's failed engage- ment since girlhood, even going so far as to strike up a friendship with Ellen Monroe, Kent's granddaughter.

"Dallas, I'm surprised to see you here." If he had been called in on a legal matter, then why was his baby sister here?

"It's Chatam House, Ash," she retorted. "They're my aunts, too."

"Of course we are, dear," Magnolia cooed in a placating fashion.

"And Ellie's my best friend," Dallas went on in a tone that a five-year-old would have punctuated by sticking out her tongue.

Ellie was the greatest surprise of all. Granted, he had last seen her on graduation day some two or three years earlier, but the pudgy, dark-haired baby doll of his memory had morphed into an astonishing beauty in that relatively short period of time. Next to his coltish sister, in her black jeans and white, long-sleeve T-shirt, Ellie looked lush in a simple, navy blue sheath belted at the waist. Her chin-length hair curled and waved about her Kewpie doll face and violet eyes. Everything about her, even her smile, seemed luxuriant.

Abruptly aware of the streaks of gray in his own chestnut-brown hair and the subtle lines that creased his forehead, Asher felt suddenly self-conscious. He had previously thought those streaks entirely suitable for a successful attorney approaching forty years of age. He'd noticed the

faint wrinkles without concern only days earlier.
Now, suddenly, they seemed ominous declarations of the fact that he was aging. His aching
knee called attention to itself at that moment, and
he very nearly turned and walked out, mentally
fabricating excuses for his aunts.

He did no such thing, of course. At thirty-
eight, he was still in his prime. Plus, he *was* a
Chatam, after all, as well as a very busy attorney,
too busy to pay attention to old aches and pains.
His sudden weariness could be attributed to this
being Friday, the end of a long week, the third in
the too-short, often dreary month of February.

"Asher, dear."

The sound of his aunt's voice recalled him to
his duty. Dropping his coat over the seat of an
armless side chair, he strode forward to leave a
kiss against her soft cheek.

"Aunt Hypatia. It's good to see you. Is there
an emergency?"

He could surely be excused for assuming such
was the case. Though the aunties were a bit out-
dated in their mannerisms and sensibilities—
Asher's father, Murdock, insisted that his older
sisters had been born a hundred years too late—
Asher had never before received a message from
them. This one had arrived, written on ivory
vellum and hand-delivered by the aunts' mid-
dle-aged factotum, Chester, only an hour earlier,

requesting his presence at Chatam House as soon after five o'clock in the afternoon as possible. Naturally he had rearranged his schedule and appeared, as summoned, at barely a quarter past the appointed hour.

"Not an emergency, per se," Hypatia answered carefully.

"There is, however, a problem," Mags added, summoning him to her side. He craned around the piecrust table and bussed her leathery cheek, then repeated the process with Odelia's plump one.

For once, Odelia, who was seated next to Mags on the settee, did not giggle. In fact, she barely smiled, nor had she yet spoken. Lovingly referred to by her nieces and nephews as Auntie Od, the woman was usually effusive to the point of silliness, which made this uncharacteristic solemnity seem ominous at best.

"What's wrong?" Asher asked.

"It's the Monroes, dear," Hypatia informed him kindly, signaling the elder Monroe with a regal wave of her hand.

"Well, you see—" Kent Monroe began.

"Our house caught fire," Ellie interjected quickly.

Some things, Asher noted wryly, had not changed. Ellie had always exhibited an unfortunate tendency to interrupt. He raised his brows at her, as he always used to do, in silent rebuke—only to tumble headlong into her wide, violet eyes. Surprised, he forced his attention back to the matter at hand.

"It's not a total loss by any means," she was going on blithely. "The smell is the worst of it, really, but that should prove no real problem. It's amazing how they have products now that can just take odors out of the air, isn't it?" She continued on about air fresheners and the unreasonable strictures of the fire department.

For an instant, Asher felt himself once more being pulled under by those dark-lashed eyes, and he realized that he was staring. He retreated swiftly to the fireplace. Parking himself there, he paused to take stock of the gathering in the huge, gilt-framed mirror above the mantle.

The first face to jump out at him from that group reflection was, of course, Ellie's. Rounded and apple-cheeked, her face seemed made of sweetness, a disturbingly adult sweetness. Her unusual coloring—pale pink skin, dark hair and sparkling violet eyes—added a sense of the ethereal to a face that could only be described as... enchanting.

He felt a strange sense of alarm. This was Ellie, for goodness' sake, little Ellie Monroe, his baby sister's best friend.

She turned sideways on the edge of her seat,

watching him with a wide, troubled gaze. He felt a sudden urge to bolt from the room. Instead, he turned and folded his arms, targeting Kent Monroe with a penetrating gaze.

"I'm sorry for your trouble. What exactly does this all mean?"

"The house is structurally sound but uninhabitable," Mr. Monroe said, glancing at Ellie apologetically.

"Which is why they are here," Magnolia put in.

Asher smiled. The aunties seemed to be making a habit of taking in strays. Over the past several months, they'd taken in no fewer than half a dozen needy souls, but he knew exactly who would be responsible for this particular state of affairs. He gave his sister a pointed, accusing glare, to which she immediately took exception.

"Don't look at me like that, Ash. Where else could they go?" She lifted her chin defiantly, tossing her short, red curls. Like him and all the Chatams, she had a cleft in that proud little chin. Hers was nothing more than a gentle dip in the center; his was more pronounced.

"And, of course, they are most welcome," Hypatia hastily said, "but I'm sure that they would like the insurance matter settled sooner rather than later."

Kent inclined his round head, saying in a gravelly voice, "You are too kind, dear lady, you and your sisters. Believe me, we want nothing more than to go home as quickly as possible and would not impose a moment longer that necessary, but the insurance company—"

"—is so impersonal," Ellie finished for him, rushing on. "You know how they are. They don't return your phone calls when you think they should, let alone write the checks. It's infuriating for him, especially after all these years of paying premiums, which is why I've taken over the whole thing." She spread her hands as if to say that the matter was settled.

Asher looked to her grandfather. "I assume that you are the policyholder." Kent nodded. "Confidentiality rules would prevent the insurance company from discussing the matter with anyone but you or—"

"I'm sure they'll settle eventually," Ellie interrupted. "These things never move as swiftly as we'd like."

"—your appointed legal representative," Asher finished doggedly.

"Ah," Magnolia said in a voice of deep satisfaction. "I knew you would agree."

Agree? Asher noted at once the look of smug approval on his aunt's face and felt a jolt. All these years of avoiding legal pitfalls, and he'd been led into a trap by a trio of little old ladies with sweet smiles and teacups. And it was a very neatly sprung trap, too.

Arguments against the Monroes taking on legal counsel, his in particular, immediately formed. Legal representation could sometimes gum up the works when it came to routine claims, and an attorney too busy to devote adequate time to the issue could well delay, rather than expedite, matters. On the other hand, well-phrased and well-timed inquiries from a legal source could work wonders.

Asher glanced at Odelia, recognizing her shaky relief, and knew he would do what he could, if only for Auntie Od. Odelia, God bless her, seemed far less comfortable than Dallas at having the Monroes as guests at Chatam House. That alone was reason enough to help settle the insurance claim.

Besides, why spend time and energy on escape when compliance would free him sooner? In fact, if he hurried, he might still be able to make his meeting.

It was a routine matter, really, the usual gathering of regional youth soccer commissioners at the beginning of a new season. He had intended to argue, once again and most likely without results, for the formal training of volunteer coaches at every level of the system. But he didn't care if he lost the argument. Soccer was his great, overriding passion. It was his buffer against a crazy world. He couldn't wait to get the season started.

He checked his watch, pushing back his French cuff. If he hurried, he could make the last few minutes of the meeting and still press his point.

"I'll look into it," he announced, smiling as he stepped away from the fireplace. "Call my secretary Monday morning with the particulars," he instructed Mr. Monroe.

Ellie sat up straight. "Oh, but—"

"I'll get back to you in a few days," he went on, walking toward the door.

"Can't you stay long enough for tea?" his sister asked pointedly.

"Sorry. I have a meeting."

He didn't quite make it across the impressive foyer before the quick tap of footsteps on marble warned him of pursuit. Dallas, no doubt. Slinging on his coat, Asher cast a glance upward issuing a brief, silent plea for patience.

Of his three siblings, his baby sister had always tried him most, so naturally she had been the one to follow him from the family home in Waco to Buffalo Creek, where she had earned a teaching degree at Buffalo Creek Bible College and remained to teach second grade. Intending to make

short work of any confrontation, he whirled—
and nearly bowled over Ellen Monroe.

She bounced off him, pinwheeling her arms to
keep from falling over backward. Instinctively,
he reached out to grasp her forearms and steady
her. A bright smile suddenly lit her face, and
electricity shot up his arms. Jolted, he snatched
his hands back.

"Sorry."

"No problem," she said, smoothing her skirt.
"I—I just wanted to…uh, thank you."

"I haven't done anything yet," he pointed out,
frowning.

"No, but you're going to," she said, "and I'm
beyond grateful. But I hate for you to put yourself out over this. I know how busy you must be,
and…" With a forced chuckle, she held out her
arms in a broad shrug. "Well, I'm sure God will
work it all out in His own good time."

Asher blinked, irritated by his odd response
to Ellie, a response he couldn't quite character-
ize. "Is it not possible that God could use *me* to
work it out?"

"Oh!" She clapped her hands to her chest
just below her delicate collarbones. "I didn't
mean—"

"Because I assure you that the insurance
company will seek every means to mitigate

their damages," he interrupted, "even if it's only delaying payment as long as possi—"

"But Dallas is always saying how busy you are, and I wouldn't want to impose."

He sighed. "You're not imposing. You're taking on legal representation." The attorney in him forced out a disclaimer. "Though, of course, I cannot guarantee that you and your grandfather will be entirely happy with the results of my actions."

Ellie flattened her lips as if disappointed. "I've found people are just about as happy as they make up their minds to be."

Life brought all sort of disappointments, as Asher knew well, unhappy and tragic things, like death and divorce, injury, malfeasance, house fires… The list, in fact, seemed endless. But perhaps she was too young to understand the harsh realities of this life, while Asher, on the other hand, had seen far too much tragedy, animosity and downright dishonesty in the course of his practice to be so sanguine.

Recently, his cousin Chandler had been cheated of his investment in a ranch. Thankfully, all had turned out well. In short order, Chandler had married, become a father and purchased another ranch near Stephenville to the west. It had all happened, Asher mused, while Chandler and his now wife, Bethany, had been living in this very house.

Come to think of it, his cousins Kaylie and Reeves had also met their spouses while one or the other of them lived here, a fact which must surely have influenced his starry-eyed little sister to seek shelter for the Monroes in this place. Was Dallas trying to get Kent and Odelia together? And was Ellen also a part of that?

If so, shame on them.

Until a person had been disappointed in love, that person could not understand the depth of pain that accompanied such disappointment. Dallas and Ellie were still too young for that kind of experience.

Feeling sadly world-weary to the point of, well, old, Asher could have used a bit of Ellie Monroe's youthful naïveté and enthusiasm just then. Instead, he smiled and brought the conversation to an abrupt end.

"Have a good evening, Ellie."

He left her there, looking like the little girl she had been not so long ago, the little girl whom he, on some level that he definitely did not wish to examine too closely, needed her still to be. He pushed the image of her lovely violet eyes aside.

He had no interest in romance. His one spectacular failure in that area had cured him permanently of any desire to meet, or date—let alone marry again.

Ellie sighed as the door closed behind Asher Chatam's back. She had always sighed upon first seeing him, and today had been no exception. For as long as she'd known his sister Dallas, some six or so years now, Ellie had thought the tall, lean attorney the finest-looking man she'd ever seen. Slim-hipped and broad-shouldered, with the build of an athlete, he seemed the very epitome of the successful barrister. She had always imagined him as a champion of the downtrodden and wrongly accused, but she knew little about his business. She adored the distinguished streaks of off-white at his temples, the warm amber of his eyes and the cleft in his strong chin.

Unfortunately, when he was around, she couldn't seem to think as clearly as usual. He made her nervous, and when she was nervous she blurted out things better left unsaid, interrupted others and often embarrassed herself. She had no reason to worry, though. He had never seemed to notice. Sadly, so far as she could tell, the man barely realized that she was alive. She was just his little sister's best friend, after all, a kindergarten teacher of limited experience. He, no doubt, fended off much more sophisticated women on a daily basis.

Nevertheless, Ellie found this turn of events intriguing. A dedicated attorney such as Ash Chatam would pay close attention to his clients, and she yearned for him to play close attention to her. But, she reminded herself, close attention could be disastrous. She had actually pleaded with the Chatam triplets not to impose on their nephew, but her entreaties had gone unheeded. In fact, the more she'd begged them not to involve Ash, the more determined they had seemed to do so, until finally they had dispatched Chester to enlist Asher's aid.

"He's definitely taking the case then?"

Ellie turned to find Dallas lounging against the staircase banister. Her friend's nonchalant pose and tone did not fool Ellie. Dallas was as concerned as Ellie herself. "Did you think he wouldn't?"

A small sigh escaped Dallas before she made a dramatic shrug. "I told you, if the aunties ask it, you might as well consider it done."

Ellie took a seat on the third step, smoothing her skirt neatly about her thighs. "Tell me again why you don't want Ash involved in this," she suggested as mildly as she could manage.

"You know perfectly well why," Dallas said, dropping down beside Ellie so she could pitch her voice low. "He'll have you and your grandfather out of Chatam House in no time, and the longer you're here, the more likely it is that your grandfather and Aunt Odelia will get back together."

"And that's the only reason?" Ellie pressed softly.

Dallas shifted her gaze away, springing to her feet. "Of course. What other reason could there be?" Dallas could never sit still, but Ellie suspected her restlessness had less to do with habit and more with…something else just now.

Ellie looked down at the marble floor.

"Gotta go, kiddo," Dallas said abruptly. She patted Ellie's shoulder and whirled away to poke her head into the parlor and call out a farewell before setting off.

Ellie watched her go with a heavy heart. Frankly, she missed her friend. The two of them usually spent hours a day talking or just hanging out, but since the fire a distance had grown between them. The fire had left so many questions in Ellie's mind, questions for which Ash Chatam would surely demand answers.

"You're looking very pensive," her grandfather noted, as he trundled through the parlor doorway and across the foyer.

"Am I? Well, it's been a busy day."

"Keep you hopping, do they, all those five- and six-year-olds?"

"Do they ever!"

"You adore them, every one," he remarked.

Ellie smiled. "They're such fun."

"Have fun with what you're doing—" Kent began.

"—and you'll never want to do anything else," Ellie finished for him.

Ruffling her curls as he had done since she'd had curls to ruffle, he started up the steps, but then he paused, his gaze going back toward the parlor. Bending, he quietly asked, "Have you noticed how subdued she is?"

Ellie didn't have to ask which "she" he meant. "Um-hm. But I wouldn't read too much into it."

Sighing, he straightened and began the long climb, muttering to himself, "A subdued Odelia is not the real Odelia."

Ellie pretended not to hear, her gaze on the bright yellow door that led out onto the front porch of the mansion, where Chatams had lived, according to Dallas, since the last brick had been laid. Even Asher had lived here for a short time long ago while his house was being built on the north side of town. She closed her eyes in dismay, once more seeking spiritual comfort.

Oh, if only the Chatam sisters had not called Ash into this mess!

It couldn't end well for any of them, not for Dallas, not for her grandfather, not even for the Chatam sisters, who had been so very kind, and certainly not for herself.

Broken hearts, she very much feared, were soon going to be the rule rather than the exception—her own among them.

Chapter Two

Shifting in her customary seat on the antique settee, Odelia stifled a sigh. The room seemed strangely vacant now that Kent had excused himself. He'd stayed only long enough to be polite after Asher had gone, but then, Kent never lingered in her presence for a moment longer than necessary. She couldn't blame him.

Who would have imagined that her former fiancé would one day take sanctuary here at Chatam House? Odelia certainly would not have, not after what she'd done to him. Perhaps time had diminished the hurt she'd dealt him, but she was only too glad to provide him a kindness now or anytime. When Dallas had first explained the situation nearly two weeks ago, the first reaction of Odelia's sisters had been to gently refuse, but Odelia herself had argued fiercely that God had His reasons for bringing the Monroes to their doorstep, and she still believed that. She just hadn't counted on how having Kent in the house would affect her.

How could it be that after all these years, some small vestige of her original feelings for the man would still be rattling around inside this old heart of hers? Now, she longed continually for his company and, though he avoided her, dreaded the day when the Monroes would move back into their house. Why, oh, why had Hypatia and Magnolia insisted on calling in Asher? Their nephew was bound to get to the bottom of things and come to terms with the insurance company in short order, and then, before she knew it, Kent would be gone again. Well, perhaps it was for the best at that.

Blanching, she looked down at her hands, ringed fingers twining together anxiously. Once, she had wanted very much to marry Kent Monroe, and had nearly done so. Only at the last moment had she realized that she could never be happy living apart from her dear sisters. But when she had suggested to Kent that they live with her family, he hadn't taken it very well, claiming that a "real man" would make his own home. She had understood that perfectly, but it had still hurt.

The aftermath of the breakup had been quite difficult for her, but she had never regretted her decision not to marry. Kent had truly been the only man who had ever tempted her to do so. When Kent had married Deirdre Billups, Odelia had put away her secret longings, and she had been more than content over the years. She had actually been quite happy and genuinely glad for Kent and Deirdre when, after years of marriage, their son had been born. Likewise, she had grieved for Kent and Deirdre when their son had died in an accident at the age of forty-one and then again, over a decade ago now, for Kent when Deirdre had succumbed to an aneurysm.

Since that time, she and Kent had gradually renewed their friendship, always keeping a polite distance. She had found that arrangement very satisfactory and had imagined that they would end their lives as casual friends with their shared past unremarked but unforgotten, at least between the two of them. Instead, in thirteen short days she had somehow reverted to her old foolish self, longing for the kind of relationship that she had long since determined was not for her. How could she, at her age, feel such nonsensical, girlish emotions? She was simply astounded.

"Dearest, are you all right?" Hypatia asked, calling Odelia from her reverie.

Odelia looked up, glancing from one sister to the other. Both watched her with concern etched upon their faces.

"Who, me?"

"Certainly she means you," Magnolia said with a snort. "Who else? *I* certainly wasn't engaged to Kent Monroe."

Odelia forced herself to laugh brightly, hoping that it didn't sound as stilted as she feared. "I'm fine! Why wouldn't I be? It's not *our* house that caught fire."

"You just seem…not yourself lately," Hypatia observed gently.

"Not yourself," Magnolia agreed.

"If having Kent Monroe here is disturbing to you—" Hypatia began.

"It could be dyspepsia," Magnolia pointed out brusquely. "You remember how Mother suffered with dyspepsia. It put her all out of sorts."

"—we could always offer to put them up in a hotel," Hypatia went on, sending Magnolia a speaking glance.

"I'm not dyspeptic!" Odelia insisted, turning on Magnolia. "I've never had digestive difficulties in my life." As her waistline must surely demonstrate, she thought morosely.

"Well, of all of us, you're most like Mother," Magnolia argued defensively.

Plump, she means, Odelia thought. Perhaps she ought to pay a bit more attention to what she ate, she decided, mumbling, "My digestion is fine."

"It's certainly not unrequited love," Magnolia commented, chuckling. "Not at our age."

Odelia frowned and batted her eyelashes against a sudden welling of tears. She might be past the age of romance, but surely she should not be past the age of caring about her weight, if only as a matter of health. Abruptly, she wondered what Kent thought about her rounded figure. He had once declared her the very model of slender femininity, but what did he think now? Had age and indulgence robbed her of all appeal?

Closing her eyes, she told herself not to bring Kent into this, not even mentally. Obviously, to her shame, she needed to pray much more diligently about her personal lapses, and so she would. Meanwhile, she'd be boiled and peeled before she'd give in to this nonsensical emotional confusion.

Mentally centering herself, she heard Hypatia say, "I understand that new hotel out on the highway is quite comfortable and even offers kitchenettes. If we phrased it delicately and prepaid, say, a month's rent, I doubt that either Kent or Ellie would take offense. We could always—"

"Oh, for pity's sake, Hypatia!" Odelia snapped, popping open her eyes. "There is no polite way to turn someone out of your home when you have already offered them shelter and have more than ample accommodations for them."

Horrified at this uncharacteristic harshness, Hypatia drew back, her eyes wide.

Beside Odelia on the settee, Magnolia drawled, "I think she should see a doctor."

Embarrassed, Odelia considered placating her sisters by agreeing, but then she thought of Brooks Leland, the family physician, and knew that he was far too astute not to see that her problem was emotional and spiritual rather than physical.

Fighting for an even, melodic tone, she said, "I don't need a doctor. I just need…" she looked to the windows at the front of the long, rectangular room "…sunshine." Rising to her feet, she continued, "I need sunshine. And fresh air. Spring. I'm so very tired of winter. I need a dose of spring." Making a beeline for the foyer, she decided that she would take an overcoat from the cloakroom and let herself out the sunroom door. "If you need me, I'll be in the greenhouse," she told her sisters. *Praying,* she added silently.

Perhaps then she could put aside these ridiculous longings and dreams, for such foolishness should be the purview of the young. What need had she of love at this late date, after all? It wasn't as if they had time for children or growing old together. They were already old, she and Kent.

Too old.

* * *

Nothing promised such new possibilities as a Monday morning. At least, Ellie had always thought so. She loved the early-morning tranquility and neatness of her classroom, the moment of sublime peace before the children began to arrive, bringing their happy chaos with them, but Monday mornings were the best. As such, they always seemed ripe for prayer, but especially this particular Monday morning.

She'd mulled the problem of Asher Chatam all weekend without finding a solution, and now, as she read over her morning's devotional, she wondered why she had not simply taken the matter to God. As the author of the devotional reminded her, God knew everything to be known about the whole situation anyway, even more than she did. He was just waiting for her to ask Him for the solution. Really, she could be so foolish sometimes. It was a wonder, a testament to God's patience, that He didn't drop stones out of Heaven onto her head at such moments.

Spreading her hands over the pages of her devotional book, she closed her eyes and began as she always did, whispering the words in her mind.

Holy Father, make me Your instrument this day. Help me to love and teach my students, to see and meet their needs as You would have me

*do. And, Lord, please show me how to deal with
this mess I've gotten myself into. My grandfather
deserves to be happy, really happy. He is the
very soul of cheerful forbearance, as You know,
and I know that Odelia would make him happy.
I'm as convinced of it as Dallas is, only I would
never have...*

She bit her lip, unwilling even to put into words
what she feared. It wasn't as if she had any proof,
after all. Besides, who was she to judge? And if
Dallas had done something foolish to bring her
aunt and Ellie's grandfather together, well, what
sense did it make to waste an opportunity like
this? Just because she wouldn't have done what
she feared Dallas had done didn't mean that God
couldn't use the situation for good. Did it?

If only the Chatam sisters hadn't brought Asher
into it! He could be a tad severe, and Dallas had
always painted him as somewhat stodgy, but even
she admitted that he was a very fine attorney, ex-
tremely intelligent and he could be trusted im-
plicitly. Sadly, while Ellie admired those traits,
they meant that he was bound to have the insurance company settling up in no time. Or worse
yet, he might discover the truth of the fire—
whatever that was—and then where would they
be?

Would the insurance company even pay if the
fire had been deliberately set? And what would

happen to her dearest friend if… She turned off that line of thought, concentrating instead on her grandfather's happiness.

Please, Lord, couldn't You intercede here, just delay things a bit, maybe? I mean, Ash is bound to be busy. He has that prosperous look about him that busy attorneys who make lots of money often—

Her thoughts came to an abrupt stop. Money. That was the answer! All she had to do was tell Ash that she and her grandfather could not afford to pay him. Surely, that would put the brakes on things.

"Thank You," she said brightly.

"For what?" asked a child's voice.

Ellie's eyes popped open. Her gently arched brows shot upward as she took in the two former pupils who stood with their bellies pressed to the front of her desk. Students often did that, especially when they wanted something. One of their mothers, a woman by the name of Ilene Riddle, stood behind them at a short distance.

"Hello," Ellie said.

"Hello, Miss Monroe," the two girls replied in sync.

"We didn't want to disturb you," put in the mother, moving forward a step. "You seemed to be meditating."

An attractive platinum blonde with white-tipped nails and dark eye makeup, she had just been divorced for the second time when her daughter, Angie, had entered Ellie's kindergarten class about a year ago now. Angie and Shawna, the second girl, had quickly become best friends and apparently still were. Ellie noticed that in contrast to her mother's neat stylishness, Angie still looked as if she'd slept in her clothes, her short, dark blond hair sticking out at odd angles.

"I like to start my day with a prayer," Ellie said, smiling. "Now, what can I do for you?"

"Please, Miss Monroe," Shawna pleaded, tilting her dark, sleek head, "we don't get a coach, and we 'membered that you can play."

"You played with us all those times at recess," Angie put in eagerly.

"Play?" Ellie echoed, puzzled. "Play what?"

"Soccer," Ms. Riddle clarified. "The girls have signed up for the spring soccer season, but there aren't enough coaches to go around. Unless we can find someone to help out, the girls won't get to play."

"Oh, dear," Ellie said, rising to her feet, her hands still planted atop the book on her desk.

"I've volunteered as team mother," Ilene went on, "but I know nothing at all about the sport. I mean, I can organize everything, but I just don't have any of the skills needed to teach the kids about the game, and the commissioner is apparently pretty strict about who is allowed to coach. We thought—hoped—you might be willing to help us."

Ellie stood speechless for a moment. She had never coached a sport in her life, but she did know the game, having played all through high school. Straightening, she folded her arms thoughtfully, one forefinger tapping her rounded chin.

"How many kids would I work with?"

"Nine is the minimum," Ilene answered. "We actually have seven right now and could use a few more. Twelve is the max at this age."

Twelve at most. Ellie looked around the room. She routinely corralled twenty-two in this small space and flattered herself that she actually taught them something worthwhile in the process. Twelve kids on an open field would be a piece of cake by comparison.

"How much time are we talking about?"

"It's nine games and twenty practices in ten weeks, so roughly twenty-five hours."

That was little more than a full day in total, spread out over more than two months. Besides, she'd always enjoyed soccer and could use the exercise. And hadn't she just asked God to show her the needs of her pupils and how to meet them?

"Sounds like fun," she decided. "Count me in."

The girls *hurrah*ed, bouncing up and down on their toes. Ilene Riddle reached past them to clasp Ellie's hands with hers, silver bracelets jangling.

"Thank you so much. I'll help every way I can, I promise. First practice is Wednesday afternoon at five-fifteen. Do you know where the field is?"

"I think so. Across the creek from the park, right?"

"Right. I'll bring all the supplies. You just bring the expertise."

"Deal," Ellie said, smiling broadly.

As the trio took their leave, Ellie dropped down onto her desk chair once more. Well, it looked like she had her work cut out for her, starting tomorrow afternoon. She'd have to brush up on coaching tactics this evening. Thankfully, with all the information online, that shouldn't be too difficult. She'd see to it tonight.

That left this afternoon to convince Asher Chatam to drop her grandfather's case and turn his attention elsewhere.

Ellie smiled. Mondays really were her favorite day of the week.

Dropping the telephone receiver into its cradle, Asher stared at the leather-trimmed blotter on his desk. He hated Mondays. Just once, he wanted to get through a Monday without some unpleasant surprise. What, he wondered, had the aunties—and, by extension, he—gotten into? So much for settling this "routine" insurance matter and getting on with his life.

Unanswered questions about the fire at the Monroe house abounded, and Ellie Monroe had apparently done everything in her power to make certain that they remained that way. According to the adjuster, Ellie's cell phone number was the only contact information that the company now had, and she'd come up with every excuse imaginable to prevent the adjuster from speaking with her grandfather. Most troubling of all, the Monroes had recently increased their coverage and moved their most precious belongings into storage. The adjuster had even hinted at a financial incentive. Something smelled, and it wasn't smoke.

Asher was making notes on his computer when his secretary buzzed him. Without taking his eyes off the screen, he hit the intercom button.

"You heading home, Barb?" A fifty-something grandmother raising a grandson, Barbara was adamant about leaving the office by five.

"In a minute. There's an Ellen Monroe here. She says it's important that she see you but promises she'll only take a few minutes of your time."

Asher sat back in his chair. Well, well. Ventured right into the lion's den, had she? Reaching forward, he shut down the computer and monitor.

"Send her in. Then get out of here and have a good evening."

"Will do. See you tomorrow."

He tightened the knot in his gold-striped tie, spun his tan leather chair to face the door and waited, hands folded. As the sound of footsteps on the polished oak floor in the hallway grew louder, Asher's heartbeat sped up. He told himself that it was his normal reaction, the old fire-in-the-belly response to a challenge. The instant Ellie appeared in the doorway, however, he knew that he was kidding himself.

Wearing a dark purple pantsuit over a rose-pink blouse, she looked absolutely lovely. She also looked distinctly uncomfortable. Intending to use that discomfort to his advantage, he found a smile and rose.

"Just who I wanted to see."

"Oh?" she said in surprise, her face lighting.

Nodding, he waved her over then watched as she folded down neatly into one of the chairs before his desk. She tucked a small handbag into the space beside her.

"Why did you want to see me?" she asked.

Sitting, he regarded her steadily. "Tell me why you're here fir—"

"You should know that we can't pay you," she blurted, suddenly looking hopeful and somber at the same time.

Asher paused, concerned. He didn't like to think it, but this information could support the idea that the Monroes had a financial motive for setting fire to their house.

She sighed, gulped and sucked in a deep breath, all telltale signs of a less-than-truthful client. Which, he reminded himself, she technically was *not;* rather, her grandfather was his client.

"Even with the insurance money," she said, "I can't imagine how we'll pay for the repairs to the house. Granddad had already sunk every penny of his savings into the renovations before the fire. I don't know what we'll do now." She went on to list numerous expenses that must evidently come before his fee.

It might be true that the Monroes were strapped for cash, but he knew a convenient dodge when he saw one, and his curiosity was now piqued. Ellie Monroe was actively attempting to derail the insurance settlement, and he meant to find out why.

"My aunts have essentially asked this of me," he told her mildly, "and when I work for family I never take—"

"But we're not family," Ellie protested, "and

you can't go around working for nothing! It wouldn't be fair. You have your own bills to pay, after all. I understand that." She bowed her head, the very picture of stoic acceptance. He didn't buy it for an instant.

Frowning, Asher leaned forward, bracing his elbows on the edge of his desk. "There's no need for you to worry about my bills, Ellie."

"So you're going to do this pro bono?" she demanded, sounding miffed. "Isn't that for charities and such?"

"Not necessarily."

While she sputtered about fairness and good faith and half a dozen other things he didn't follow, he mulled his options. He could throw her out—she wasn't his client and therefore had no say in his employment. On the other hand, her reasons for derailing the settlement could range from merely misguided to serious malfeasance. And, because she was not his client, he had no way to protect her in either case. He decided he would do his best to keep her out of trouble. She was his sister's friend and a tenant at Chatam House, which meant that he had represented her as well as her grandfather.

His decision made, he pulled open a side drawer, took out a receipt pad and flipped it open.

"If it will make you feel better," he interrupted, "then by all means, pay me."

"But I just told you that—"

"How much cash do you have on you?"

For a long moment, she said nothing. Asher sat back in his chair, enjoying the moment. For once, he had reduced Ellie Monroe to speechlessness.

"What?" she finally squawked.

"How much cash do you have on you?" he repeated slowly.

Frowning, she pulled her purse into her lap. "Seven or eight dollars, maybe."

"Let's make it a buck, then," he said, leaning forward to scribble out the receipt. "No, two. One for you, one for your grandfather." He made certain to write both of their names on the correct line. After tearing the receipt out of the book, he tossed the pad back into the drawer and nudged it closed.

"You can't mean to represent us for two dollars."

"It's that or nothing," he retorted with a shrug. "You're the one who wanted to pay me. Call it a retainer, if it makes you feel better."

Frowning, she reluctantly laid two crumpled dollar bills on the desk. He swiftly traded the receipt for them and slipped them into his shirt pocket. "That takes care of that."

She made a face. "Look, even if your aunts did drag you into this, I don't expect you to knock yourself out settling our little insurance claim, not for two bucks."

He smiled. "I have a question for you." He folded his arms atop his desk blotter. "Why are you trying to get me off this case?"

Shock flashed across her face, followed swiftly by guilt. "I—I don't know what you mean."

"Tell me what you're hiding."

"What makes you think I'm h-hiding something?" she hedged, averting her gaze.

"This isn't my first day on the job," he pointed out, hardening himself against those suddenly woeful eyes. "And you're a terrible liar."

"I'm not lying!"

"You're stalling the insurance company," he accused in his most lawyerly voice. "Why?"

Biting her lip, she shook her head. "You don't understand."

"I'm trying to, because I can't help you if I don't know why you're doing this!" He leaned toward her. "Is it your goal to remain at Chatam House indefinitely?"

She broke, blurting, "I only want my grandfather and your aunt to have a chance to get together!" She quickly clapped her hand over her mouth.

"I knew it!" Asher cried, smacking a hand against the desktop. The lawyer in him crowed, even while the annoyed nephew was exasperated.

But Asher Chatam, who had known Ellie for quite some time, was worried.

He now had at least a part of the truth.

He wasn't at all sure, though, that he wanted the rest of it. Because he wasn't sure that he could protect her—not if her foolishness was as great as he feared.

Chapter Three

She had told him! She had told Asher of her deepest hope, despite Dallas having warned her that he would be appalled, even offended, at the very suggestion of Odelia and Kent rekindling their romance. Ellie suddenly feared what else she might tell him if he pressed hard enough.

"I need to know everything about the fire, Ellie," he said in a soothing voice that she dared not trust, not after the grilling she'd just endured. "Tell me about that night."

Dismay filled her, followed quickly by irritation that she'd let herself be cornered like that. She shifted in her seat, crossed her legs and hemmed and hawed before finally telling the story.

She and her grandfather had moved a quantity of furniture into storage to make room for the workmen who were renovating their seventy-year-old house. As the work progressed, they had replaced one room's furnishings with that of the next, swapping out contents as the necessary renovations were completed.

"They did the roof first, then moved inside, starting upstairs," she told him. "They were ready to move downstairs to the bedroom that had been my grandmother's, so we took her antique French Empire bed suite to storage that night. It's easily worth more than everything else in the house put together, and Grandpa takes good care of it, calls it part of my legacy."

Asher's brown eyes regarded her intensely. "Go on."

Ellie took a deep breath and explained that she and her grandfather were still trying to fit the bed suite into the rented space without damaging it when Dallas had arrived. Asher's brows rose as she repeated the story that Dallas had told her. Out jogging that evening, Dallas had stopped by the Monroe house on impulse to discuss a date Ellie had gone on the previous night. Dallas had ostensibly seen the fire through the front window. She waved down a passerby, who happened to be Garrett Willows, the gardener at Chatam House, as he drove down the street on his motorcycle.

Willows had called 911. The Fire Department

had arrived within moments and put out the fire a short while later. That was apparently when Dallas remembered that Ellie and her grandfather were moving furniture into storage that night. Willows had offered to take her there so she could break the news in person. That was also when she'd called her aunts, who had immediately offered sanctuary.

"And that's all there is to it," Ellie said, not quite meeting his gaze.

"And how did the fire start?"

She gulped, then made herself look at him, noticing that as she did so his gaze dropped to her lips. "Apparently a can of paint remover spilled, then a hot lamp tipped over, the one we always left on when we were away from the house at night." She shrugged and looked down at her hands. "I don't know how it happened in an empty house. Someone said there was a loud noise, like a car backfiring nearby."

"And you think something like that could have knocked over a can of paint remover and a lamp?" he asked skeptically.

"There could have been a collision at the track yard," she insisted. "The switching lane is just a few hundred yards from the house. It isn't used much, but when it is, we can feel it, almost like the ground is moving."

"But if your theory is correct," he mused, "then the paint remover had to be open when it tipped."

"The workmen sometimes just set the cap on the neck and didn't screw it down until they were done," she told him. "They warned me about an open can more than once when I came into the room where they were."

Asher leaned back in his chair. "Plausible," he admitted, but his tone implied that he found it just barely so.

He stroked a fingertip over the cleft in his chin. "You, ah, mentioned going on a date the previous evening."

Ellie blinked at the change in subject. "What about it?"

"Just wondering if you've broken anyone's heart lately."

She scoffed, laughing. "Hardly."

"There hasn't been anyone special then?"

"I wish," she quipped. "What there have been are a lot of first dates, emphasis on the word *first,* as in not many *second* dates." She wrinkled her nose. "I just don't seem to find any keepers, if you take my meaning. Dallas says I'm too picky, but I notice that she doesn't have a steady boyfriend, either."

He smiled then abruptly sobered again. "By any

chance, might one of those first dates have been with Garrett Willows?" he asked carefully.

Ellie blinked and frowned, shaking her head. "I never met him before that night. Why?"

"I'm just trying to understand the overall situation."

"But I've told you what happened."

"You put forward a supposition," he pointed out, "but you've as good as said that you don't really *know* what happened."

She slid to the edge of her seat and laid a hand on his desktop beseechingly. "Look, however it happened, it wasn't malicious."

Asher beetled his brow. "And how do you—"

"It just stands to reason," she said too quickly. "I mean, it's not as if we have enemies."

"Then who set the fire, Ellie?"

"I don't know!" she shot back. And she didn't. Not for sure. "No one! It was an accident."

"Did you arrange that fire to promote a romance between our relatives?" he demanded.

She gasped. He suspected her? Here she was trying to protect his beloved but harebrained sister, and he would put the blame on *her?* Indignant, she rose to place both hands on his desk. Leaning forward, she brought her face close to his, so close that she could smell the minty freshness of his breath. "I had absolutely nothing to do with that fire!"

"Nothing?" he asked skeptically.

"Zip," she declared flatly, punctuating her denial with taps of her forefinger against his blotter. "Nada. Nil. Zero. Zilch. I didn't set it! I didn't cause it! I didn't have anyone else do it! I didn't know it was going to happen. I still can't believe that it has!"

After a very long moment, Asher relaxed back in his chair. "I had to ask," he said, as if that excused all.

Sighing, Ellie dropped her head. He believed her. He believed that she had nothing to do with the fire, and in that moment, fool that she was, that was all that mattered.

Asher still had serious questions, but he felt sure that whatever had happened, Ellie had not purposefully caused the fire at the Monroe house. Deeply relieved, he smiled. She blinked and smiled back. For a long moment he couldn't look away. Then another thought came to mind. Though she might not have been responsible for the fire, she was certainly guilty of meddling in other people's lives.

"So you didn't start the fire, but you're not above using it for your own purposes," he accused, frowning.

She dropped down onto the edge of the chair again. "My grandfather taught me that God doesn't let anything into the lives of His children without a reason, and getting together two people who care about each other seems like a pretty good one to me."

"Please," Asher scoffed. "Odelia and your grandfather haven't had feelings for each other in fifty years."

"You don't know that."

"Even if they did have feelings for each another, I would discourage them from entering into a relationship at this late date. It isn't sensible."

Ellie gasped. "You can't be that cold!"

That, surprisingly, stung. Coldness was what his ex-wife, Samantha, had accused him of when her tears had not moved him. Perhaps if she had not employed them after making angry demands, he would have been more amenable. Perhaps she wouldn't have left him then. Perhaps his wouldn't have been the first divorce in his family. He blocked further thoughts on the matter.

"I'm simply pragmatic," he refuted, keeping his voice level. "Two people the age of your grandfather and my aunt ought not become entangled romantically. It's just not wise, fiscally, emotionally or in any other way."

Ellie narrowed her wide, violet eyes at him.

"Just because they're older, you think they don't deserve to be happy? How hard-hearted can you be?"

Asher felt his temper begin to spike. "I never said they don't deserve to be happy."

"Just that they should ignore their feelings for each other!" Ellie exclaimed.

"You don't know that they have feelings for each other any more than I know they don't!" he pointed out.

"Well, we won't know whether they do or not if we don't give them a chance to find out, will we?"

"What difference does it make at this point?" he demanded. "They're past the point of contemplating children or building a financial future together."

"Love and marriage are about more than children and finances! It's about companionship and emotional support."

"Oh, please! It's not as if either of them is living a lonely, barren existence. Aunt Odelia has her sisters. Your grandfather has you."

"But what about tenderness, satisfaction, the fulfillment of a heart's desire?"

Asher rolled his eyes. "Believe me, it is entirely possible to live without those things. In some ways, it is even preferable."

Ellie fell back into her chair, staring at him

with those breathtaking eyes. To his horror, tears welled up. "That's the saddest thing I've ever heard," she told him in a soft, trembling voice.

He gaped at her, his chest tightening, and felt the urge to rush around the desk, slip an arm about her shoulders and apologize. Then he realized that she'd manipulated him exactly as Samantha had always done. His anger abruptly turned outward again, though he did his best to subdue it with reason.

"Sad?" he echoed. "But that's just what I'm trying to tell you. Life without romance is not necessarily unhappy. In fact, it can be infinitely more comfortable. Believe me, I know."

"You poor thing," she whispered, her expression melting into compassion. "Who was she? Who was it who broke your heart?"

Asher's jaw dropped as his ex-wife's face flashed before his mind's eye. He saw her on their wedding day, resplendent in her white dress, even then, impatience and disappointment stamped on her face. He had ignored that, knowing that he had been less engaged in the planning and process of the wedding than she would have liked. He'd told himself that once he finished law school and passed the bar, things would settle down, but he'd soon realized that she expected more than he could ever deliver, more time, more attention, more emotion. He remembered the contempt on her face the day that she'd declared him hopeless and asked him to leave their apartment.

Quickly banishing the memories, Asher told himself yet again that the divorce had been the best thing. The marriage had been the mistake. At least he and Samantha had seen the error of their ways before they'd brought children into it. God had taught him a valuable lesson with the failure of his marriage—that his career and personality would leave him neither the time nor the inclination for love and romance.

He had since come to find that such things were not necessary. In fact, given all the acrimonious divorces that he'd seen, Asher did not understand why any mature person entertained notions of romance.

"You misunderstand," he began, reclaiming his composure, only to have Ellie interrupt.

"God can heal a broken heart, you know," she told him gently.

"Yes, of course, but—"

"But you must allow Him to do it," she counseled. "You must be willing."

Exasperated, Asher muttered, "It's not a matter of—"

"Because He surely has some lucky woman picked out for you," Ellie plowed on, not allowing him to complete so much as a sentence. "She's waiting right now, the one woman in the world who will treasure everything about you."

He lifted his eyebrows at that. "Oh, really?" he quipped with equal parts intrigue and ridicule.

She nodded, smiling. "She'll admire all your sterling qualities."

"Sterling," he mimicked, amused now. She was beginning to sound like his aunts. Obviously, the old girls were rubbing off on her. "I've always wondered. What exactly is a 'sterling quality'?"

She sat back in her chair as if surprised that he had to ask. "Well, in your case, confidence, kindness—"

"You told me I was hard-hearted a moment ago," he pointed out drily.

"I was wrong," she admitted with ease. "I said that without thinking, before I knew you'd been hurt."

He opened his mouth to tell her that he had not been hurt but he found he couldn't quite make the words come out.

"A hard-hearted man would not take on a case just because his aunts asked him to. Plus, you're intelligent and good at what you do, successful, respected, honest and you obviously value family. That's all very important to women, you know. And, of course, you're handsome."

"Handsome," he repeated, realizing only belatedly that he was starting to sound like a parrot.

"The graying at the temples is very distinguished," she went on, tilting her head. "Though it's not really gray, is it? It's more of a champagne color, I think. Very unique."

He suddenly couldn't think of anything sensible to say. "I, uh…" He shifted uncomfortably in his chair. "Um…thank you."

She beamed so brightly that her whole being seemed to shine. His lungs locked, refusing to allow air in or out. Then she ducked her head and confessed, "You have gorgeous eyes."

The reality of the situation slapped him fully in the face. She was flirting with him! His world tilted, leaving him clinging to the very edge of reason. Abruptly, he saw himself falling into that sanity-stealing violet gaze, and his every instinct demanded that he flee to safety. He was halfway to his feet when she bounced up, declaring that her grandfather was waiting for her at the pharmacy across the street.

"Ah." Not exactly an intelligent observation, but it would have to do. He threw an arm toward the door, wordlessly inviting Ellie to take her leave.

She rose smoothly and walked toward the door. He hung back, snatching his jacket from the rack and throwing it on. His overcoat followed that, yet he somehow managed to catch up with her in the doorway.

Pausing there, she turned and lifted a dainty hand to brush across his striped tie. "Just think about what I said," she whispered before moving off down the hallway.

Asher stared at her retreating figure for a long moment before he shut his eyes. No, no, he must not think about her…uh, about what she'd said. What had she said?

The door in the waiting area opened and closed, signaling that she had left the premises. He sagged against the door frame, shaking his head and sucking in huge drafts of air.

What on earth was going on? He had sworn off the fairer sex, and he'd been perfectly happy in his solitary existence. Besides, he couldn't be attracted to Ellie Monroe. Not only was she now officially a client, she was twenty-three, too impulsive, too talkative, too…everything!

Especially too pretty.

Why, the woman was downright dangerous. Oh, she might look as innocent as lambs and sweet enough to decay teeth, but that woman was poisonous to the male population, and henceforth, he told himself sternly, he would not forget that fact. He would be on his guard—stern, disciplined, wise—just as a man in his position ought to be.

But something told him that being on his guard might not be enough to combat the charms of Ellie Monroe.

Mentally kicking herself with every step, Ellie descended the stairs outside Asher's office to the ground floor below. She loved these old art deco buildings, but she saw nothing of her surroundings as recriminations piled on, crowding out everything else.

Could she have made a bigger fool of herself? She should have realized that Asher was not handling this case for the money. He was doing a favor for his aunts. Most likely, he would not have taken on the situation at all except at their behest. Informing him of her and her grandfather's limited means to pay had probably even insulted Asher, and that was the last thing she'd wanted.

To make matters even worse, she had shown her hand. He knew that she wanted him to drop or stall the settlement and why—or partly why. Hopefully, he would be satisfied with that.

The saddest revelation of all, though, had to do with Ash himself. The very idea that he had given up on romance broke her heart, for him and for all the women out there who begged God on their knees for such a man, herself included. As a Chatam, he would be a responsible, fiercely loyal and faithful Christian husband, much like her beloved grandfather. Ellie liked to think that her own father would have been such a man, too, but Chart Monroe had died in a helicopter crash while on a training mission with his military unit when she was only ten years old. His death had driven Ellie's unhappy grandmother into bitterness and her spoiled mother into paroxysms of self-pity.

Ellie had soon learned that just as she could not depend on her mother or grandmother to help her through her father's loss, neither could she make up for his absence, so she had clung to her good-natured grandfather. Not yet thirteen when her querulous grandmother had suddenly died, Ellie had naturally turned to him for support and comfort during their mutual time of grief, and that, her mother had declared before packing up and disappearing, was just where she belonged.

Her mother's abandonment had hurt, but leaving Ellie with her grandfather was perhaps the greatest kindness that Sonia had ever given her daughter. Ellie owed so much to that wonderful old man. For years, he had bravely smiled in the face of criticism and coldness from his wife. He had been as devastated as she by their son's passing, perhaps more so, but somewhere along the way, Kent Monroe had learned to make his own happiness. He had taught Ellie to do the same.

Just once, though, Ellie wanted her grandfather to actually have his heart's desire, and she wasn't about to apologize for that, not even to Ash, who had obviously allowed his own disappointment to warp his judgment about such things.

Pushing through a heavy glass door, Ellie stepped out onto the sidewalk of the downtown square that framed the Buffalo Creek courthouse. Pausing to toss on her jacket, she spied Lance Ripley coming toward her.

She had done her best to avoid Lance after their date on Valentine's Day. It was not an easy task. As coworkers, they taught in the same building, but while she loved teaching and enjoyed children, Lance, she had discovered, despised both. He had told her bluntly that he would continue to teach only until one of his unlikely inventions sold, the latest of which was a backpack containing an air bag. Ellie shuddered at the idea of school hallways filled with exploding air bags as children did what came naturally, bumping, shoving and jabbing each other.

Lance called out to her even as she quickly turned in the opposite direction. "Ellie!"

Sighing inwardly, she resigned herself and put on a smile before slowly facing him. He strode up to her, hunching inside his rumpled trench coat. His tall frame seemed to fold in upon itself as if unable to support the shock of wheat-blond hair that sprouted from his scalp, too thick to part or comb down without a proper styling. One of those men who could have been truly handsome with just a bit of attention to the details of grooming, he had once struck her as a bundle of possibilities. Now, he represented every dating disappointment she'd ever experienced.

"I've been wanting to talk to you." The pale blue eyes that pinned her from beneath the line of a shaggy unibrow seemed oddly calculating, but she forced a tight smile anyway.

"Hello, Lance. I've been, um, busy."

"Not too busy for me, though, I'm sure," he insisted, sliding an arm across her shoulders.

Ellie stepped aside, frowning at his familiarity. They'd shared a single date, for pity's sake, and she'd regretted it long before their dinners had arrived. He'd asked her out a full week in advance, and she'd been happy to accept. She'd dressed carefully, twisting up her hair and donning one of her favorite dresses, only to find that he hadn't even bothered to make reservations. After driving all over town, they'd wound up eating burgers in a joint frequented primarily by loud teenagers while he droned on and on about his invention. She'd avoided his good-night kiss after that and his calls ever since.

"Actually," she told him, "this is not a good

time. I've got to run. Sorry." She attempted to step away, but his hand shot out and fastened around her arm.

"Now, hang on," he said, frowning.

Ellie glanced around meaningfully, but Lance seemed not to realize that they were on the verge of a very public scene. "Please let go of me."

"You've been avoiding me for the past week or more," he accused, as if she had not realized that fact, "and I want to talk."

"Lance, I don't have time for this," she began firmly, but he cut her off.

"Those old ladies you live with, the Chatams, they might be interested in investing in my safety pack. I didn't get a chance to meet them last time, so I thought I could come by sometime soon and do that."

He'd picked her up at Chatam House for their date. Thankfully, the Chatam sisters had been out at the time; otherwise, he might have hit them up for investment funds right then and there! Alarmed to think that he would try to use their tenuous connection to importune the Chatams, Ellie glared up at him.

"Absolutely not! My grandfather and I are just guests at Chatam House. We've only been here for a couple of weeks. I wouldn't feel comfortable having my own company come over."

"Huh," he said, as if the niceties of such things had never occurred to him. "But I'm not really company. We're dating."

"No, Lance, we're not," she stated flatly, drawing herself up straight. "And I really have to go."

Scowling, he gave her arm a shake. At that precise moment, Asher pushed through the door of the building and stepped out onto the sidewalk. Barely glancing at Lance Ripley, he walked over, calmly took Ellie's arm in his, breaking Lance's grasp, and turned her toward her grandfather's pharmacy.

"Excuse us," he said over his shoulder, propelling her down the sidewalk. "Mr. Monroe is waiting."

Stunned, Ellie glanced back at Lance. He brought his hands to his hips and glowered but did not seem inclined to follow. "I'll phone you," he called, as if that alone would prompt her to take his calls when she had not done so thus far.

"You can try," she muttered, swinging her smile up at Asher. She couldn't help a tiny thrill of appreciation. It really was rather gallant, the way he had swooped in and swept her away.

My hero, she thought with a melodramatic, inward sigh. If only she could believe he'd meant something personal by it. But of course, given his feelings about romance, that was out of the question. Entirely.

Chapter Four

Of all the stupid, ill-advised things to do! Asher scolded himself sternly, all but shoving Ellie Monroe along at his side. He glanced down at her worshipful gaze and inwardly groaned. If he was not mistaken, the girl had a crush on him already, and he had just added fuel to that fire. Nothing could come of it, of course. He was old enough to be…well, fifteen years her senior.

A decade and a half.

Good grief, he'd been learning to drive when she was born! But did that stop him from riding to her rescue like a knight of old? Nooo.

Yet, what else could he have done? He had come down the stairs intending to turn to the back of the building and walk right out into the alley where, as usual, he had parked his SUV. Then he'd caught sight of Ellie and that man through the front glass. Within moments, Asher had realized that the idiot had put his hands on her and that she was not particularly welcoming the familiarity. He hadn't really thought at all after that. Before he'd even known what he intended to do, he was doing it.

"One of your 'first dates,' I assume?" Asher muttered.

"A first and *only* date," she answered.

"He seemed anxious for a repeat performance."

"But not for the reason you may think."

"Oh?"

"He wants your aunts to invest in one of his inventions."

Asher stopped short of the corner and looked down at her. "Inventions?"

"A backpack with an air bag." He blinked slowly at that. She made an expression somewhere between a grimace and a grin. "To guard against pedestrian accidents."

"Pedestrian accidents," he muttered, shaking his head. Glancing back over his shoulder, he ushered her forward once more. "Doesn't exactly take a hint, does he?"

"He's still there?"

"Afraid so."

Thankfully, the light changed before they reached the corner. Asher all but pushed her across the street, and they wound up in front of the door to her grandfather's pharmacy. The lettering on the front window read, "Monroe's Modern Pharmacy and Old-Fashioned Soda Fountain."

"Thank you," she said.

Nodding, he glanced back down the street, frowning. "Maybe I'd better have a word with our inventor."

She caught him by the arm before he could turn away. "Uh, why don't I treat you to a root beer float, instead. He'll leave after we go inside."

Asher lifted his eyebrows. "A root beer float? I haven't had a root beer float since...actually, I'm not sure I've ever had a root beer float."

"Well, it's about time you did, then," she told him, pulling him through the door with her.

He went along because, really, what else was he going to do? Dig in his heels like a recalcitrant four-year-old?

Redolent of peppermint, the shop spread out in a straightforward manner, with a single cash register and short counter at the front perpendicular to the door. Rows of products ran horizontally through the center of the store, providing a clear line of vision from the glassed-in prescription counter at the back.

"Hey, sugar! Be with you in a minute," Kent Monroe's gravelly voice called out.

"It's okay, Grandpa," Ellie answered, tugging

Asher toward the candy-striped counter along the far wall. "We're going to have a treat."

"Help yourselves."

It had been ages since Asher had parked himself on one of those small, round stools at the soda bar. He usually visited one of the specialty coffee shops on the square these days. Something about those red vinyl-covered seats edged in chrome and fixed atop a stationary metal pole made him feel silly. Still, he sat when Ellie motioned him to it. She rounded the corner and slid behind the counter.

"Now, let's see," she said, looking around her, "maybe you'd prefer something other than a float. Say, a cream fizz or a sarsaparilla?"

"Really?" he said, leaning his elbows on the counter. "A sarsaparilla? No, I don't think so."

"Well, then?"

"Maybe you'd better choose."

She smiled. "A float it is, but a very special one."

He watched doubtfully as she squirted a measure of dark syrup into a tall metal cup, added a firm scoop of vanilla ice cream, blended the ingredients and then divided the resulting sludge between two tall, fluted goblets. She flooded the goblets with cola from one of the fountain taps, forming an impressive lather on each. Plucking two straws from a container, she shoved them into the goblets and carried both around the counter, where she took a seat next to Asher, facing backward.

"A cappuccino root beer float," she announced, plunking his down in front of him. Hanging her elbow on the counter, she took a long pull on her straw then drawled in a thick, syrupy voice, "For the sophisticated palate."

Asher didn't know whether to be amused or wary. He took a careful sip and arched his eyebrows, surprised by the rich flavor. "Mmm, that's good."

"It is," she agreed, spinning around on the stool so that they faced the same direction, "and terribly addicting. I limit myself strictly to five a week."

He sputtered a chuckle around his straw. "You're kidding."

"I couldn't get through that door back there if I had five of these a week. A girl can dream, though, can't she?"

"Is that what you dream of?" Asher asked offhandedly, helping himself to a napkin from a dispenser.

"No, not really," she answered, suddenly serious. She stirred the drink with her straw, drawing languid circles in the thick foam. "I dream of what every woman dreams of. Husband, home, children. Romance."

"Romance," he echoed sourly, with a shake of his head. "Romance will wreck the other three, if you're not careful."

"Is that what happened to your marriage?" she asked softly. "She wanted romance to go along with the home and husband?"

That came surprisingly close to the truth—so close, in fact, that Asher heard himself say, "Life is not romance. It's a lot of hard work and, if you're very blessed, part pleasure."

"And that's it?"

"That's all I've ever had time for."

"But what about other things, like children?"

"We didn't get that far," he said tersely, "but I can't imagine that adding kids to the mix would make room for romance."

"I think your definition of romance is too narrow," she told him. "You're talking about grand gestures of the flowers-and-mood-music sort. Sometimes romance is just knowing that you'll be together at the end of the day. It's *wanting* to be together even when the demands of life necessarily separate you."

"According to her, the 'demands of life,' as you put it, was the only part that I was any good at."

"Maybe she wasn't any good at some of her parts, either."

"What makes you say that?" he asked, shooting Ellie a surprised look. "She seems to have done okay the second time around."

"Maybe she has more in common with her husband this time, or maybe he doesn't have to work as hard as most. A wife has to be supportive of a hardworking husband."

"Even if it means giving up what she wants and needs?"

"Why would it?"

"Maybe he just doesn't have time for her. What then?"

"Then he doesn't really care for her."

He stared at Ellie, his worst fear laid bare.

"Look," Ellie said, shifting closer and lowering her voice, "every couple has to learn to make time for each other. Sometimes, one or both has to give up something, but normally they do it through shared interests and goals."

Asher stared at his drink. He could have given up soccer. At the time, it had seemed like the only thing keeping him sane, the only way he could get through law school and come home to Samantha with anything less than a snarl on his face. When they'd been dating, Samantha had often come out to watch and cheer him on when he'd played, but after the wedding, she had lost interest and come to resent every moment that he'd spent playing. But he hadn't been willing to give it up. It had seemed unthinkable, frankly.

What did that say about him as a person, let alone a husband?

"Do you still love her?" Ellie asked, watching him closely.

He wasn't entirely sure now that he had ever loved Samantha, but he simply shook his head and went with the short answer. "No."

"Then it's the failure that destroys you," Ellie surmised.

Astonished, Asher set his glass down with a plunk. He stared at her for a long moment, wondering just exactly what it was that he saw in her eyes. Understanding? Sadness? Wisdom? Hope? Something more, something from which he instinctively shied.

"I expect Mr. Inventor has gone on his way by now," he said, injecting just the right note of avuncular humor into his tone. "Gotta run." He took a last drag on his straw—the drink really was quite good—spun his stool and left, leaving her with a smile and a nod of thanks.

He didn't pretend that he wasn't running away, because he was. And he counted it among the wisest things he'd ever done.

Lord, heal that man, Ellie prayed, as Asher walked away. It wasn't as simple as a broken heart; she saw that now. The poor man had chosen the wrong woman, and he'd taken on the full blame for the failure of the marriage, but his ex had chosen wrong, too. It wasn't all his fault. Somehow, he had to learn to forgive and trust himself again. *Open his eyes, Lord,* she whispered in her heart, and then, because she couldn't stop herself, *Let him see what's right in front of him.*

Her grandfather trundled up to her. His footsteps were no longer as quick or sure as they had once been, and his belly strained against the buttons of his white lab coat, but he was still himself—a man with a huge, loving heart. She smiled in gratitude for all he was to her, all he'd taught her.

"Asher didn't stay long," he remarked.

"He's a busy man."

"The best ones are." She said nothing to that, just smiled. "Ready?" he asked.

She popped up off the stool. "Just let me wash these glasses first."

He squeezed in behind the counter and helped her. Seconds later, they left the building together. Relieved to find that Lance had, indeed, gone away, she happily allowed her grandfather to escort her to her red truck. His old sedan was constantly being serviced or repaired, so she often gave him a ride to or from the shop.

Ten minutes later, Ellie turned her pickup between the thick brick pillars at the foot of the drive, passing by the wrought-iron gate with a tall, golden *C* at its center. As she downshifted to make the slight incline, a sense of peace enveloped her. This wasn't home, and it didn't feel like home, but it did feel like sanctuary.

About halfway up the hill, the drive curved into a broad circle, with the graceful mansion standing at its apex. It was a beautiful old house, flanked by a rose arbor on the east and an enormous magnolia tree on the west. Everything about the place evoked a sense of permanence, continuity and hope.

Parking at the foot of the broad, redbrick walkway, Ellie paused to silently thank God for the safety, comfort and peace that she and her grandfather had found in this place.

"It's a special house, isn't it?" Kent remarked. "It always has been a special place because the people in it are special. Funny how we imbue a place with our essence. I think that's why there is nothing sadder than an empty house." He shifted in his seat, looking at her. "Have you ever noticed how quickly an empty house deteriorates? You can sit there for decades and do little to nothing to maintain the place, and it will eventually fall down around your ears. But walk away, leave it empty, and it'll go to pot in a matter of months, weeks sometimes."

"I hope this house is never empty," she said.

"Not until Jesus comes again and makes all things new. And even then I hope there will be Chatams here."

It was a sweet thought, one that humbled her. How silly she was to try to handle every little problem herself when the God of Creation and the Savior of Souls was in charge. From now on, she decided, she would let Him handle things and confine her own involvement to prayer. If Dallas had done what Ellie had feared she had, Ellie didn't even want to know because she didn't want to lie, even if it meant protecting her well-meaning but foolish friend. Besides, Ellie could not change anything that had happened or convince Asher to give her grandfather and his aunt time to search their hearts for long-buried feelings. Only God could do that.

Besides, being in Asher's company awoke foolish dreams. Why embarrass herself and feed her foolishness? He was not the man who could give her what she wanted, needed and deserved. He didn't even believe himself capable of being a good husband, and didn't want to try.

Perhaps it wasn't even about Asher, though. Perhaps it was all about her.

Perhaps no man was right for her. Perhaps God intended her to remain single.

Better that than married to the wrong man.

It was only later, as she settled into her comfortable bed there in Chatam House, that a thought struck her. Asher had not always thought himself a poor candidate for marriage. Obviously, he had wanted to marry at one time. Otherwise, he would not have done so. No, it was just as she'd thought earlier. He had chosen the wrong woman, and that had changed his outlook entirely. Might the right woman change it once again?

There you go, she scolded herself, punching her pillow into a more comfortable shape, *asking for trouble. Imagining yourself with Asher will only set you up for disappointment.*

It would definitely be better to avoid the temptation of spinning dreams around Asher Chatam, which meant avoiding the man himself. God would bring the right man to her in His own good time. He had never failed to provide her with anything else, after all. She could trust Him for her own happiness, as well as her grandfather's.

It was past time that she acted like it.

"Asher, dear!" Hypatia tilted her head to receive his kiss on her cheek. "We weren't expecting to see you again so soon."

Glancing meaningfully at his sister on the settee next to their Aunt Magnolia in the front parlor of Chatam House, Asher fixed a smile in place. "Well, I was told that I could find my sister here." Run her to ground, more like.

She had dodged him repeatedly over the past twenty-four hours. He'd been forced to go by the elementary school where she taught, only to be told by a coworker of hers that she'd mentioned having dinner with her aunts. He'd decided to drop by Chatam House and corner her here. Besides, he wanted a chance to get the story from Garrett Willows, the aunties' gardener.

"You'll stay for dinner, of course," Magnolia stated, exactly as Asher expected.

"Oh, say you will," Hypatia urged before he could respond.

"Absolutely," he agreed, noticing his little sister's frown.

He had to judge for himself whether Dallas knew something that Ellie wasn't telling him about the fire at the Monroe house. After all, he could not in good conscience hand off the case to another attorney until he knew what he might be handing off.

He had determined in the midst of a long, restless night that he definitely had to shed the case. And Ellie. Even if it meant paying the costs himself, though he'd make sure no one ever realized that.

The whole idea smacked of skullduggery, but

he just didn't see any other way to handle things since Ellie had made him that root beer cappuccino float and effectively laid bare his soul. He just needed enough information to make sure that he picked the right attorney to take over. Otherwise, the aunts would carve out his heart with their dainty silver teaspoons.

That wasn't the only reason he needed to see Dallas, though. The matter of his sister's meddling had to be addressed.

"Dallas, dear, will you tell Hilda that we need an extra plate laid at the dinner table?" Hypatia asked sweetly.

"Sure." Leaping to her feet, Dallas tossed Asher a sour look, her short red curls bouncing.

As she left the room, he took her seat next to Magnolia, asking, "Where is everyone?"

Magnolia revealed that Odelia had taken a walk and the Monroes had gone back to their house to put out food for their cat. "They rarely come down until dinner is on the table, anyway," she said.

Asher felt a bit of relief. He wanted to judge their reactions to his last conversation with Ellie, but he didn't want to spend any more time with her than necessary.

"They try so hard not to impose," Hypatia told him softly.

"And Aunt Odelia? Is she well?"

"Well enough," Hypatia replied, glancing away.

"She's dieting," Mags hissed, her disapproval clear.

"You're kidding!" he blurted out.

"Won't even take a decent tea," Mags told him in a low tone of voice.

Asher frowned. Could it be because of Kent Monroe? He shook his head. A younger woman might seek to lose weight in order to impress a man, but a woman of Odelia's age? He couldn't believe it. On the other hand, she had grown rather round in the past few years. Perhaps it was a simple matter of ill-fitting clothes.

He suddenly remembered an old photograph of Odelia in a strapless ball gown. Her chestnut hair swept up in an elegant style, diamonds at her earlobes and throat, she had worn a corsage tied about one wrist and a beaming smile. Beside her, Hypatia might have traded places with the queen of England, while Mags had resembled nothing so much as a farm girl in her mother's Sunday best. Odelia, however, could have been a movie star to rival the likes of Ginger Rogers.

Perhaps having a young woman in the house— a woman as lovely as Ellie Monroe—had inspired Odelia to reclaim her figure.

He cleared his throat and tried to get his

thoughts off Ellie, asking, "Is Garrett Willows around?"

Magnolia raised her eyebrows at him. "I expect he's in the greenhouse. Why do you ask?"

Asher served up as much truth as he was willing to at this point. "I've never had the opportunity to talk to him. Just thought we might be able to connect over the dinner table."

"Oh, no, dear. Garrett doesn't eat with us very often now that his sister has moved out of the house," Hypatia told him.

"I don't know why," Mags groused. "The boy's not just staff now. He's practically family!"

"Young men need time to themselves," Hypatia told her.

Mags merely *humphed* at that. Her fondness for the fellow spoke well of him, but Asher believed in forming his own opinions, and Willows had more than the usual number of variables to assess. He forgot for the moment that Willows and the Monroes would soon be someone else's problem.

Hypatia changed the subject to Asher's parents, and they chatted about his father's plans to retire at last from his practice. Surgery, Asher pointed out, was a complex matter requiring constant reeducation, and his dad had just turned sixty-nine. At sixty-one, his mother intended to continue seeing pediatric patients several days a week, but she had recently taken on a much younger partner.

"Do you think they'll move home when your mother fully retires?" Hypatia asked hopefully.

Asher smiled. "I wouldn't count on it."

His parents had lived in Waco for thirty years. Though their ties to Buffalo Creek were strong, he didn't see them moving back here anytime soon. His mother had hinted that the advent of grandchildren in their lives could change that, but Asher had told her in no uncertain terms to look to his younger siblings, none of whom were married yet. Phillip, thirty-one, lived in Seattle and pretty much kept to himself, answering phone messages with texts and the occasional email, often weeks after the fact. No one was even entirely sure what he did for a living, though one thing was certain: like the rest of the siblings, it was not connected to the field of medicine. Petra, at twenty-five, still lived with their parents while finishing her master's degree in hotel management. That left Dallas, who was in her second year of teaching—and her twenty-third year of meddling, which was why the Monroes were now ensconced in Chatam House and disrupting his life.

In fact, if Dallas had not purposefully set out

to make the acquaintance of Kent Monroe's granddaughter, she would not even be friends with Ellie and he would have been spared the inconvenience of…an unwanted attraction. Dallas had announced her intention to introduce herself to the Monroes on the very day that she had first arrived on campus at Buffalo Creek Bible College. As her much older brother, Asher had always taken a rather parental role with Dallas, so he hadn't hesitated to caution his sister not to interfere in something that did not concern her, but as usual she had not listened.

Over time, Asher had relaxed about the situation somewhat. For one thing, she and Ellie seemed to have developed a genuine friendship. For another, Dallas obviously had not made much progress in her campaign to rekindle a romance that had been dead for nearly half a century. He'd known from the beginning that Dallas's romantic obsession with their aunt's failed engagement was going to prove catastrophic in the end; he just hadn't anticipated that the catastrophe would somehow involve him.

Laughter suddenly echoed in the foyer. Recognition shivered through Asher. Though he was quite certain that he had never heard Ellie laugh like that, he knew it was her. He recognized her on a visceral level, as if some part of her had invaded his subconscious. Staying where he was took every iota of his willpower. But he didn't know if his impulse was to run away—or run toward her.

Chapter Five

"You make fun," Kent Monroe said, trudging into the parlor, "but I've always wanted a tree house, and now seems a good time to go for it."

"I don't think Grandmother's French Empire bedroom suite will fit up in a tree," Ellie noted wryly, following behind him.

Kent stopped in his tracks, sighed dramatically and slumped his shoulders. "Well, so much for that. Another dream bites the dust."

Coming up beside him, Ellie looped her arms about his shoulders, counseling softly, "Never give up your dreams, Grandpa. It's not too late."

Kent smiled, patted her forearm and quoted, "Where there's life, there's hope."

"Exactly."

A throat cleared, and Ellie looked around just as Asher rose to his feet. Kent smiled and boomed a hearty welcome, but Ellie's first feeling was dismay. How was she to keep her distance from Asher when he could pop up at Chatam House at any moment? She quickly smoothed her features and nodded in greeting.

"Any news?" Kent asked of Asher.

"Uh, no. Sorry. I'm simply here to have dinner with my aunts."

"I thought you wanted to speak to Dallas," Mags said.

"That, too." He looked at Ellie. She quickly glanced away. Kent sent her toward an armless side chair before plodding over to drop down into the empty armchair next to the settee.

"And how is your pet?" Hypatia asked him as soon as he was seated.

Asher waited until Ellie sat before resuming his own seat. She smoothed the skirt of the royal blue minidress that she wore over matching leggings and flat, ankle boots.

"Still haven't seen old Curly," Kent said, "but at least he's eating."

"Or something is," Ellie put in. "We really have no way of knowing if it's the cat or something else. We just put out the feed, and it disappears."

"An opossum could be eating it," Magnolia commented, "or a skunk."

"Mice even, maybe," Ellie said. "We keep the

cat food bag on the enclosed mud porch, and something has torn a hole in it."

"Guess I'll have to do a thorough search for my poor old tom," Kent said. "He must be traumatized by all that's happened, and it can't help that we're not around for him to come home to."

Ellie sent her grandfather a sympathetic smile. "I'm sure he's fine. He always did like to roam, you know."

Kent nodded. Dallas appeared in the wide doorway between the foyer and the parlor just then, announcing, "Hilda says to come to the table."

"Oh, but Odelia isn't here," Kent protested, glancing around the room as if making certain that he hadn't missed her.

"Yes, she is," Dallas said, flashing a smile at him. "She's waiting in the dining room."

Kent hauled himself to his feet and swiftly lumbered into the foyer. Dallas stepped aside to let him pass, targeting Asher with a self-satisfied look. He flashed her an irritated glance, then smoothly came to his feet as Ellie and his aunts did. Ellie brushed her hands over her skirt and swiftly moved forward. It was going to be an interesting evening. She meant to keep her head down and her mouth shut; she could only hope that Dallas would do the same.

* * *

Asher stepped toward the door, hot on Ellie's heels, only to feel a hand catch at his elbow. He looked down to find Magnolia gazing up at him, her gray braid lying upon her shoulder and brushing against the notched collar of her shirtwaist dress. Of course. How could he have forgotten, as Kent obviously had, that his very proper aunts would expect a gentleman to provide them escort to the table?

Dutifully, he offered one arm to her and the other to Hypatia. Smiling graciously, his dear old aunties flanked him, and they began a stately progression. Ahead of them, Ellie and Dallas walked close together, their heads bent in quiet conversation. As they moved toward the dining room, Asher couldn't help comparing his sister and her friend.

Dallas looked boyish in her slender jeans and skinny black turtleneck sweater, while Ellie... well, even in her heyday Ginger Rogers had had nothing on Ellie Monroe.

Asher admitted to himself that he might have misstepped by coming here like this. He'd had little opportunity to speak with his sister in private thus far, and Garrett Willows seemed likewise unavailable, so all he'd really accomplished by getting himself invited to dinner was to throw himself into company with Ellie Monroe, which was the last thing he should have been doing.

Determined afresh to concentrate on the matter at hand, he glanced down at his aunties, only to find them sharing a knowing look. Asher felt his face heat. He had just been caught staring at Ellie Monroe. And for that he was going to rip his little sister to shreds. Just as soon as he managed to corner her. If she had just cooperated… but then, when had Dallas ever? Well, he could be stubborn, too.

Biding his time throughout dinner, Asher struggled to observe his sister and ignore Ellie, with little success. Though she sat on the opposite side of the long table and several seats farther down than he did, Asher couldn't help noticing the gusto with which Ellie enjoyed her meal. And the way she constantly smiled. At everyone but him. That rankled more than it should have, and despite his better judgment he found himself purposefully engaging her.

"So, how did you find the odor at the house today, Ellie? Still overpowering?"

"We didn't go into the house itself," she reported with a frown. "The firemen blocked the doors."

"Though what the holdup is on getting the blocks taken down, I can't imagine," Kent put in from his seat at the foot of the table. "Ah, well, makes little difference. It's not like any-thing is going to change until the insurance com-pany ponies up." Smiling, he looked to Odelia as if expecting confirmation of his assessment. Odelia, however, was staring at her plate with a woebegone expression.

Troubled by what her sisters had told him ear-lier, Asher asked, "Don't you like the pasta, Aunt Odelia?"

She looked up in surprise. "What?"

"You're not eating," he pointed out. "Is the pasta not to your liking?"

"Of course it is," she said, giving him that sweet smile before quickly forking a bite into her mouth. "Delicious."

"It is," Asher agreed. "One of Hilda's best dishes, which is saying something." He meant to let the matter end there, but instead he heard himself saying, "Ellie certainly likes it."

She instantly dropped her fork, her face col-oring. Too late, he realized how that must have sounded, as if he thought she was eating too much. And he couldn't think of a way to smooth it over. Everything that came to mind would only make it worse.

I don't think you're a pig.

I like a woman with a hearty appetite.

You look great to me, so don't even think about going on a diet.

Ellie turned to Hypatia, saying quietly, "Hilda is an excellent cook."

"We're very blessed to have her," Hypatia agreed.

"This is so good that I'm quite full already," Ellie went on softly, "so if you'll excuse me..."

"Oh, of course, dear." Hypatia smiled politely then glanced at Asher.

Ellie pushed her chair away from the table, stood and left the room.

Obviously, his thoughtless comment had driven her away. Mortified, Asher bent his head and continued to eat, only to discover that his own appetite had gone with her. He put down his fork and picked up his glass of iced tea, telling himself that he should be glad she'd left the room. But he didn't feel that way at all. Frustrated, he fought not to follow Ellie, bouncing his knee beneath the table, an old habit he'd thought mastered long ago.

Dallas stood next, saying, "No dessert for me, either. I'll just pop into the kitchen and thank Hilda before I head out." She started off but Magnolia hailed her.

"Dallas, dear, would you mind running out to the greenhouse? If Garrett is still there, tell him to stop what he's doing and come in to dinner."

Dallas smiled. "I'll see to it."

Doubly frustrated now, Asher once more

watched Dallas leave on an errand for his aunties, while Magnolia muttered about Garrett working too hard and being stubborn. Quickly, Asher, too, excused himself.

"Isn't anyone staying for dessert?" Hypatia asked in an exasperated tone.

"Maybe I'll have some later," Asher told her with an apologetic smile.

As he made for the door, Asher heard Kent declare that he was looking forward to dessert. Asher didn't linger to hear more. Instead, he hurried after his sister, down the hall and into the sunroom at the back of the house. Weaving his way through the wicker furnishings, he let himself out the French doors onto the patio. The greenhouse stood in the distance. The glass-paned walls of the sizable structure, though lit from inside, were fogged. Still, he could see a shadowy figure moving about at the rear of the building.

Asher sprinted across the yard, dodging mulched flowerbeds devoid of blossoms and the occasional strategically placed bench. The cold of winter had yielded to a gradual warming in past days, inspiring Asher to leave his coat in his office. The evenings remained crisp, however, leaving him grateful for the lack of wind and even the insufficient weight of his suit jacket.

Before he could reach the greenhouse door, a

tall, muscular man stepped out. Wearing comfortable jeans, heavy work boots and a dark T-shirt under a denim jacket, he brushed something from his coal-black hair, hunched his shoulders and started toward the carriage house behind the mansion where the staff—Chester and his wife, Hilda, her sister, Carol, and the gardener—lived. This, then, had to be the latter.

"Willows, is it?" Asher said, picking up his speed and putting out his hand.

The man stopped, his expression inscrutable in the deep shadows of night. "And you are?" He kept his hands in his jacket pocket.

"Asher Chatam. Nephew."

Willows withdrew a hand from a pocket and offered it for a shake, saying, "The lawyer." The tone of his voice made it clear what he thought of that particular breed, so Asher didn't make polite conversation but instead got straight to the point.

"I have some questions about the fire at the Monroe house and your involvement in it."

The hand went back into the pocket. "Didn't have any involvement in the fire. I was riding down the street on my motorcycle when this redhead in a jogging suit dashed out in front of me, waving her arms like a crazy woman. I managed not to run her down. She pointed out the fire, I phoned 911 and, since she said no one was inside, waited until they got there and put the thing out. Whole thing didn't take twenty minutes. Then, when I realized she was a Chatam, I gave her a ride to the storage unit. She stayed with the Monroes. I came back here. Then later, they all wound up here. No surprise in that, I guess. Every stray in town seems to wind up here sooner or later. Myself included. Most of this is in my statement to the authorities, by the way."

Asher frowned, uncertain whether he liked or trusted this fellow. He seemed awfully flip for a convicted felon on parole. Everyone in town knew the story of how he'd gone to prison for beating his stepfather, who by all accounts had been a brutal man and murdered Garrett's mother. No one in the family had been especially pleased when Magnolia had hired Garrett. Deciding to ignore that last statement, Asher went back to the beginning.

"So you were just riding down Charter Street, on your way where exactly?"

He felt, rather than saw, the fellow's smirk. "Church."

On Thursday? Asher thought. The fire had happened on the first Thursday in February. "Which church?"

"Downtown Bible. Same as you, I imagine, though I haven't seen you, not at the late service and not at the monthly men's Bible study."

Asher tried not to let his irritation show. "And you're a regular attendee of that Bible study, are you?"

"Not yet. It just started in January, and I missed February. For obvious reasons."

"How long have you known the Monroes?"

"Since the night of the fire."

"And Dallas?"

"Since the night of the fire."

"But you stopped for her anyway?"

"It was that or run over her. I almost laid down the bike as it was."

"So you're just the Good Samaritan in all this?"

Willows said nothing to that, just stood there, a big, silent shadow in the dark. Asher's frown deepened. They stood about the same height, but the other man's bulk made him seem larger, tougher—and somehow not particularly trustworthy. Still, his story pretty much jibed with Ellie's. So far. Cold prickled Asher's skin, but he'd have turned into a human Popsicle before he'd have let on.

"Okay. Thanks. I know where to find you if I have any more questions."

Willows nodded but before he started off again, Asher jerked his head toward the greenhouse. "My sister in there?"

"Your sister?"

"Dallas."

That came as an obvious surprise to the man. He took a half step back, his hands sinking farther into his pockets. "No. Ellie is, though."

It was Asher's turn to be surprised. "I thought my sister was supposed to be coming out here to remind you that it's time to eat."

"Don't know about that," Willows said, walking off toward the carriage house, "but like I told Ellie, I'll eat as soon as I wash up."

Asher stood staring at the door to the greenhouse. He warred with himself, torn between running after Dallas, who had obviously sent Ellie out here in her place, and finding out just how well Ellie Monroe had gotten to know Garrett Willows since coming to Chatam House. Or maybe they were both lying and they had known each other for some time—long enough to plan an arson, say. Asher didn't really believe that. Then again, he didn't know what he believed anymore.

Striding forward, he wrenched open the door. Moist, welcome warmth flowed over him. Rows of rough wooden tables stacked with tiered shelves of potted plants in various stages of bloom lined both long walls. Larger plants, some that would decorate the patio in more sultry weather, filled the interior of the long, narrow building, including a number of small trees that seemed about to outgrow their space.

Asher came to a space enclosed in heavy plastic sheeting, split down the middle to allow access. Slipping through, he glanced around at tables laden with tiny pots of seedlings basking beneath the benevolent light of long, hooded lamps. A figure turned from a shadowy corner, a figure he would know anywhere.

"Ellie."

At the same time she asked, "Garrett?"

"Where's Dallas?" he asked, not bothering to correct her because her recoil at the sound of his voice had signaled her recognition.

"She said she had to leave and asked me to deliver a message to Garrett for Magnolia."

Asher snorted at that. "Did you tell her that I know about your little plot to embroil my aunt in a romance with your grandfather?"

"Yes, of course."

Of course. So, Dallas knew that the jig was up, and she was making herself scarce to avoid a scolding. No doubt she was gone by now. Pushing back the sides of his jacket, he parked his hands at his hips and shook his head.

Well, this need not be a wasted opportunity. In this private setting, he could tell Ellie that he had decided to hand off the case. He could say that he didn't have time to give the matter the attention that it needed or even that another attorney had more experience with insurance companies, which would be true as soon as he found someone like that.

A little voice inside his head asked if he really wanted to hand off the case, and he had to admit that he did not. What he really wanted was to get to the bottom of this situation and see it resolved happily for all involved. Looking at Ellie standing there in the soft light of those heat lamps, he wondered if that was even possible, especially for him. Whatever happened, no matter how this turned out, he was going to come away from this with a sense of discontent.

He didn't precisely know why that was so. He only knew that nothing would ever quite be the same again.

Fidgeting nervously, Ellie considered her options. She had promised herself that she would avoid Asher. He had to know that she admired him, but he obviously did not return the sentiment. He'd implied, in fact, that she was an overeater, and he'd done it in the same tone that she'd heard him take with Dallas—a light, brotherly voice seasoned with a pinch of patronization and a dash of criticism, not that she could blame him. She was a little round, and she did enjoy a good meal. Since coming to Chatam House, she'd enjoyed far too many of them, in fact, and he had obviously noticed.

"I'm sorry if I upset you earlier. I didn't mean to imply…that is, I wouldn't want you to think that I think you're too—"

"It's all right. I know I'm chunky."

He looked up sharply. "You're not chunky. You're…"

She wasn't about to argue the point. "Okay, I'm too curvy then."

"No, Ellie, you're perfect. That is, your shape is perfect. Not that you aren't personally. I—I mean, I wouldn't know that, but I can see…" He winced, lifting a hand to the back of his neck.

Swamped with delight, Ellie stood there with her mouth open for several seconds.

He looked up at the glass ceiling. "Surely," he said through his teeth, "I don't have to tell you that you're very attractive."

"Really?"

Sighing, he bent his head and pressed the fingertips of his left hand to the space between his eyes, as if his head hurt.

"Are you okay?" she asked after a moment, concerned even though she couldn't seem to stop smiling.

"Fine," he croaked. "I'm fine." He waved his hand without looking at her, turned and said, "I should be going."

"Wait." Emboldened by his compliment, she stepped forward to lay a hand upon his arm. He froze. "I should apologize to you, too."

He finally looked at her. "For what?"

"Yesterday. I snapped at you."

"Well, I essentially cross-examined you."

She blinked. "That's what you do, cross-examine people. That's to be expected, but I called you cold and hard-hearted."

"Believe me, I've been called worse," he said with a lopsided smile.

She frowned, hating to think of him being called ugly names, but then she remembered something more important. Looking deeply into his eyes, she lifted her free hand to his shoulder. "Have you thought about what I said?"

"Uh…"

"You can't give up!" she exclaimed.

He shook his head as if confused. "Give up on what?"

"Romance! Love." He groaned, but she barreled on, "God is just waiting to heal your broken heart, and I know that love is out there for you. No one understands better than I do how difficult it is to have faith about this. I've been looking for the right guy my whole life, with zero results thus far. But I know that God will bring him to me when He's ready, when I'm ready."

He rolled his eyes, frowning. "You're too young to even be thinking about settling down—"

"This isn't about me. It's about you. Don't you want children?"

"I—"

"You must. Think what a wonderful father you'd be."

His brows drew together in a pained expression. "You don't know that."

"Yes, I do. Why wouldn't you be?"

He shook his head. "You have to be a good husband before you can be a good father, and I'm not husband material."

"Don't be silly!"

"Listen, I tried marriage, and I wasn't any good at it."

"Then she wasn't the right woman for you," Ellie insisted. "You just need the right woman."

He stared at her for so long that she began to feel foolish. When his gaze dropped to her lips, her heart started to thunder. For one insane moment, she thought he was about to kiss her. She tilted her head and was on the very verge of going up on tiptoe when the door to the greenhouse thumped open.

Asher jerked back as if she'd suddenly burst into flame, shock contorting his face.

She had been right in what she'd said. All he needed was the right woman.

But that woman was not—and could never be—her.

Chapter Six

Following quietly as Asher slid through the heavy plastic sheet dividing the building, Ellie tried to quell her disappointment. This was precisely why she should avoid him. When she was around the man, she imagined all sorts of improbable scenarios! He was hazardous to her sanity, and now that she'd said her piece, she would definitely keep her distance.

That shouldn't be too difficult after tonight. She was sure he'd want to avoid her now for fear that she'd read too much into his compliment. She understood now, of course, that it was just part and parcel of his apology.

Still, she would treasure his words.

"That's Odelia," Asher muttered, parting the branches of a small tree. He angled his shoulders as if about to push through the potted forest toward his aunt, but just then the door opened again and Kent came inside.

Quickly, Ellie grabbed Asher by the arm and tugged him back. Maybe her time hadn't come yet, but she believed with all her heart that her grandfather's had. When Asher looked at her, confused, she lifted a finger to her lips.

"Are you all right, Odelia? You don't seem well."

Odelia twittered, but the laughter sounded forced to Ellie's ears. "Thank you for asking, but I'm fine. Just needed a breath of fresh air."

"You came out without your coat," he pointed out.

"Oh, but it's wonderfully warm in here, don't you think?"

"I suppose it is."

She laughed again, that nervous, birdlike twitter that could not have sounded more uncomfortable. Kent sighed audibly.

"Odelia," he said, "I wouldn't willingly cause you a single moment of distress. Perhaps Ellie and I should find somewhere else to go."

"Don't be silly!" Odelia retorted, much too brightly. "Why would your being here distress me? I'm just feeling my age this winter."

"Pish-posh," Kent refuted heartily. "You are ageless, my dear, as beautiful, vivacious and adorable as ever."

"Oh!" Odelia squeaked. "Oh, my!" With that, she fled the greenhouse.

Kent sighed once more. Ellie gently parted the limbs in time to see him follow Odelia out, sadly shaking his head. She turned at once to Asher.

"See? There's still something between them."

"That's not how it seems to me. He may be carrying a torch for her, but she obviously wants nothing to do with him," he said.

"Of course she does! How could she not?"

Asher folded his arms. "Look, I'm sure your grandfather's a great guy, but Odelia declined to marry him once, and she doesn't seem too keen on a flirt—"

"My grandpa's not a flirt!" Ellie protested, insulted on his behalf.

Asher pinched the bridge of his nose. "Just once, could you not interrupt?"

Ellie recoiled. "I didn't realize that I was. I don't usually."

"Not only do you interrupt, you finish other people's sentences."

Wounded, Ellie concentrated on breathing steadily. Blinking her eyelashes to keep the tears at bay, she gulped. "I—I never mean to do that, and it's only when y-you're around." Suddenly realizing what she'd just said, she couldn't bear another moment in his presence. "Excuse me," she whispered, plowing through the trees toward the door.

"Ellie!" he called, crashing behind her.

She pushed through the door and ran for the house, barely feeling the sting of the February chill. The door of the greenhouse slammed but she didn't slow or look back.

"Ellie!" he called again. Then, just as she reached the house, he muttered. "Oh, what's the use? I'm wasting my time."

The words carried clearly over the cold night air. Wasting his time. He thought her a waste of time.

Ellie pulled open the French door and rushed into the sunroom. Dashing her hands across her eyes, she pulled herself together, lifted her chin and crossed the room to step into the hallway, which was mercifully empty. Despite her best efforts, however, tears were rolling from her eyes by the time she reached the privacy of her room.

"Of all the idiotic, ill-advised, inept…" Asher grit his teeth against further invective, mentally kicking himself as he strode around the great house. He'd be hanged if he'd follow her inside and try to apologize—again—in front of his aunts. Not after almost kissing the girl!

What on earth had possessed him to stay in that shadowy, private space with her anyway? He couldn't even make a sensible, decent apology when she was around.

Surely, I don't have to tell you that you're very attractive.

Surely, he should have his head examined for saying such a thing! Except, she honestly hadn't seemed to know.

What was that about anyway? Hadn't any of those clods she'd dated told her?

He picked up his pace, only to nearly mow down someone hiding in the shadows, someone small and plump and wearing too much flowery perfume.

"Aunt Odelia," he gasped, clasping his arms about her to steady her.

"Oh. Asher," she said, trying to hide her sniffling.

"What are you doing out here?" he asked.

"J-just taking a walk," she warbled.

But they both knew it was too cold for a walk. That was why she'd gone to the greenhouse to begin with.

"What's wrong?" he asked.

"What m-makes you think there's anything wr-wrong?"

"You're crying!" he exclaimed. "Is this about the Monroes? If it is, I'll have them out of here by dark tomorrow."

"No!" Odelia gasped, her hands clamping onto his forearm. "You mustn't!"

"But if Mr. Monroe's presence here is—"

"Don't you see?" she wailed. "This may be all I ever have! When he goes again, he may never come back."

Asher's jaw dropped. Then she shivered, and he quickly slipped out of his suit coat to drape it about her shoulders. As she murmured thanks, he turned her and walked her toward the front of the house. Gathering his thoughts, he ushered her across the thick, brown cushion of grass to the redbrick walkway, then turned her toward the front porch.

"Let me get this straight," he said, climbing the few steps beside her. They walked to the trio of wrought-iron chairs placed to one side of the bright yellow door. With their cushions stored away for the winter, the chairs were stiff and cold, but Odelia sank right down onto the nearest one. Asher took the chair beside her, clasping her frail hand in his. "You don't want the Monroes to leave?"

She shook her head then nodded and finally sighed. "That's right. I don't want them to leave."

"Especially not Kent Monroe," Asher probed gently.

She parked her elbow on the arm of the chair and dropped her forehead into her palm. "I never stopped caring for him, you know. I just couldn't leave my sisters." She looked up at him then with wide, liquid eyes, adding woefully, "No matter how handsome and charming he is."

Good grief, Asher thought, dumbfounded. *Ellie and Dallas are right.*

"You won't tell, will you?" Odelia asked urgently. "I know he doesn't feel the same way, and I don't want my sisters to think they're responsible for anything. Because I chose them, I mean."

"I won't tell," Asher promised. Still, he hated to see his sweet auntie so bereft. "But what makes you think he doesn't feel the same?"

"Well, he married, didn't he?"

Surely, she hadn't expected the man to pine for fifty years. On the other hand, perhaps she had. And perhaps he did. "He seems pretty smitten to me," Asher muttered beneath his breath.

"Oh, no," Odelia refuted firmly. "That's just his way. So charming."

Asher opened his mouth to ask what she meant by that, but then he thought of the unanswered questions about the fire. Odelia didn't deserve to get caught up in that. Besides, what were the chances that anything would come of this? The Monroes would eventually move out and the aunties would go on as always. Wouldn't they? Patting her hand, he mumbled, "I'm sure it'll all work out."

"Yes, of course," she agreed, nodding her head decisively. "God will take care of everything in time. In truth, I'm grateful to Him. I never thought to have these weeks, you know."

Asher didn't know what to say to that. A chill raced across his shoulders then, and he rose, drawing his aunt up with him. "It's too cold for you out here. I want you to go inside and ask for a nice, hot cup of tea."

Odelia smiled. "Excellent idea. You always know what's best to do, dear."

He wished. Her confidence in him humbled him, however. He walked her to the door, received his coat, kissed her cheek and saw her inside before turning toward his SUV, wishing heartily that he had never come here this evening.

How had he let himself get dragged into this mess? Henceforth, he decided, he would limit his involvement to pressuring the insurance company and keep his distance from Chatam House and the Monroes. With the spring soccer season about to start, that shouldn't be too difficult, since his time would be at a premium.

Why that thought didn't comfort him, he didn't even want to know. Meanwhile, he would ask his cousin Chandler about Garrett Willows and get a better read on the fellow that way. Beyond that, he didn't know what else to do.

Poor Odelia, he thought. She was deluded about not one but two men—Kent Monroe and him.

Why, Asher wondered, gripping his cell phone almost hard enough to crush it, had he thought that his cousin Chandler would be impartial when it came to Garrett Willows? The man was Chandler's brother-in-law, for pity's sake. Of course he would have only good things to say about his wife's brother.

Chandler had quite a bit to say about Kent Monroe and Ellie, too. Had Asher realized how well Chandler knew them, he'd have been more careful about his own comments, but no, he'd had to shoot off his mouth about Ellie's ridiculous romanticism. At least he had enough sense to keep mum about the scheme to get Odelia and Kent together, but that didn't keep Chandler from laughing at the notion that either of the Monroes or Garrett Willows might have had anything to do with the fire, and wondering aloud if Asher had more than a "professional" interest in Ellie.

"The girl is fifteen years younger than me!" Asher protested.

"So what?" Chandler retorted. "You're both adults."

"Not to mention," Asher ground out, "that we're total opposites."

"You know what they say about opposites attracting."

"Plus, she's a client," Asher pointed out incredulously.

"You're entirely too rigid about that stuff," Chandler chided. "You need to loosen up. Smiling Ellie might be good for you."

"Smiling Ellie?"

"Sure. Haven't you noticed? She's always smiling. Kent, too. It's one of the things I like best about them."

Always smiling, Asher thought sourly, pinching the bridge of his nose, *except around me.* That might have to do with the fact that he continually found ways to insult her.

He wasn't usually so ham-handed with people. He'd walked that fine line for years, the line between probing and speculating, implying and accusing. Yet, with Ellie he always seemed to say the wrong thing. Shame dogging him, he remembered the look in her eyes before she'd run away the night before. He should have followed her, but how could he when he obviously couldn't trust himself around her? Really, he had no choice but to stay away.

He changed the subject to Chandler's family and listened to Chandler gush happily about the joys of marriage and fatherhood. Though he was glad to know that his cousin was so happy, the conversation did nothing to help Asher with the Monroe case. He felt a bit depressed when the call finally ended.

What a perfect waste of a Wednesday afternoon, Asher thought in disgust. He pulled his office door closed behind him as went out, pausing only to lock up. The weather had turned unseasonably warm, with temperatures rising into the sixties. A good day for soccer, then, even if not for him.

Today was the deadline for coaching assignments, which meant that he would have to disappoint at least one team. He didn't look forward to telling a group of eager first graders that they didn't have the adult volunteers or players to qualify for competition, but he really had no choice. Rules were rules, after all, and while they might yet recruit enough players to field a team, the team couldn't play without a qualified coach, no matter how much they or he might wish otherwise.

Ten minutes later, he parked his SUV, shrugged off his suit jacket and surveyed the athletic field. Green was beginning to sprout in the carpet of winter-brown grass.

Three teams were milling around in front of three different goals. A few parents in lawn chairs had taken up seats on the sidelines. He recognized two coaches, one of whom balanced a soccer ball against one hip. The other team was scattered, with kids running around flinging dirt and grass clippings at one another while a blonde woman in jeans and a brown jacket sat watching from a rough bench, a bright orange cooler on the ground beside her. This, he assumed, was Ilene Riddle, the team mother who had vowed to find a coach, without success, apparently. They had spoken on the telephone but had not yet met.

As Asher strode toward her, he pulled his black referee's cap from his rear pocket and fitted it to his head.

Only the letters "BCYSA" emblazoned on the front in yellow-gold letters, the acronym for Buffalo Creek Youth Soccer Association, set him apart from the other referees, who wore plain black. The blonde woman turned her head as he drew near, and he put out his hand as he heard a vehicle pull into the graveled parking area behind him.

"Ms. Riddle?"

"Yes."

"Asher Chatam, soccer commissioner."

She hopped to her feet and slid her hand into his, her white-tipped nails lightly scoring his wrist. "Nice to meet you." They shook before he parked his hands at his waist.

"I see that you haven't found a coach."

"Oh, we have."

Asher lifted his brows. "Really? That's good news. Where is he?"

"She," Ilene Riddle corrected, pointing, "is right there."

Asher turned. And couldn't believe his eyes.

Ellie Monroe closed the door of a pickup driven by her grandfather. Wearing pink shorts and an overlarge, black, long-sleeve T-shirt, she had pulled back her curly hair in a short, jaunty ponytail. Waving goodbye to her grandfather, she turned toward the field and started forward at a jog, only to falter when she met his gaze.

"Asher?" she asked, coming to stop before him. "What are you doing here?"

Try as he might, he could not help but admire those violet eyes again. "You're the coach?"

Nodding, she answered, "Yes, but why are you here?"

"I'm the commissioner," he said, not sure whether to laugh or yell in frustration.

She gawked for a moment, then threw out her hands. "Dallas mentioned that you played soccer in college, but I had no idea you were still involved in the game."

He'd hardly viewed what he was doing as being "involved in the game." It wasn't the way he'd hoped to be involved, anyway, but that was beside the point. Her involvement was the issue here. "Have you ever played?"

"Fourteen seasons," she told him proudly, "from the time I was four years old straight through high school."

Well, that's just wonderful, he thought sardonically, wanting to tear out his hair. How was he supposed to keep his distance from her now? Desperate, he began shooting questions at her, testing her acumen. She didn't miss a beat. Her violet eyes sparkled so brightly that Asher had to look away. When she started arguing for the Dutch Model, which focuses on foot drills, he all but gave up, despite his own conviction that the physical education class mode worked best for young children who didn't take instruction particularly well or possess sufficient dexterity for skill-based coaching.

"That doesn't mean it shouldn't be fun, of course," she babbled on enthusiastically, "and I've got some ideas about that, too."

"You'll have to pass a background check," he growled, already resigned to the fact his plans to stay away from her had failed, plain and simple.

"I'm a schoolteacher," she reminded him cheerfully. "I've already passed a background check. It's an unfortunate necessity for anyone who works with children."

"The time commitment is significant," he ground out.

"Nineteen more practices and nine games over ten weeks," she acknowledged with a dismissive wave of one hand.

"You understand that the team could still be disbanded if you don't meet the league minimum of nine players within the next week?"

"I've put the word out at school that we're looking for kids who want to play."

Asher sighed. "I'll get the forms you need to sign."

"Great!"

"Great," he muttered, trudging toward his vehicle for his clipboard and papers.

Ellie called together her team and introduced herself, though most already knew her—and, judging by the hugs she got from her players, liked her.

She put them in two facing rows and started them kicking balls to each other up and down the line. They missed more than they connected, but they kept at it even while she stepped aside to look over and sign the forms.

"I'll leave a few recruitment forms with Ms. Riddle, but you can download and print others if you need—"

"I already have," she told him cheerfully.

He slid the forms beneath the spring clip,

feeling that she had somehow gotten a step ahead of him. "I'll get a copy of your background check from the school and make sure it doesn't need updating. There's a meeting on Saturday morning that you are required to—"

"Just tell me when and where."

He grit his teeth and forced out the words. "Nine. My house."

She smiled. "Can I bring anything? Doughnuts, maybe?"

He stared at her stupidly. It had never occurred to him to serve anything more than coffee at these meetings.

A child shrieked with laughter, and Ellie glanced over her shoulder, saying, "I'd better get back to the team." She turned away, calling, "See you Saturday."

"Saturday," he acknowledged.

The first of many in the coming weeks, apparently.

"Lord, help me," he whispered fervently.

Ellie's racing heart made her feel slightly lightheaded. The thought that Ash was the soccer commissioner circled round and round inside her mind even as she went through the motions of drilling the kids. What did it mean? She had prayed and prayed about conquering these inconvenient feelings that she had for him, and avoiding his company had seemed the natural first step, but that idea had just been shot out the window. Asher was the soccer commissioner!

Should she back out of coaching?

Nope, she decided. Not an option. She'd given her word. Besides, this had come to her out of the blue. God had to have a purpose for that.

She would not dare to hope that His purpose had anything to do with romance—not hers, anyway.

Ah. There it was. This obviously had to do with her grandfather and Odelia. And Asher himself, of course. What a joy it would be to bring her grandfather and Odelia together! But to see Asher once more embrace the possibility of love and marriage...

She ignored the pang in her chest and lifted her thoughts Heavenward, falling back on a familiar phrase. *Holy Father, make me Your instrument. In this and in all else. I want what You want, and I trust You to bring me what is best, even if that's not what I imagine it to be. Change my heart to comply with Your will. And heal Ash's heart so that he might say the same. In the name of Christ Jesus, I pray.*

Feeling a little calmer, she did her best to concentrate on the task at hand, but it was difficult, since she had developed a kind of radar where Asher Chatam was concerned. She seemed

to know just where he was at all times, even
when he was across the field talking to another
coach.

It was all she could do not to follow him with
her eyes everywhere that he went.

Chapter Seven

While Ellie went about drilling her players, Asher spoke to the other two coaches, reminding them of the mandatory Saturday meeting. He noted quite a few envious glances tossed toward Ellie's players, who were laughing and chasing down balls like the neophytes they were. Asher figured he'd better stick around in case she needed a few tips. He could always use the time to return phone calls that he hadn't gotten to that afternoon.

He strolled along the sidelines, one eye on Ellie and her team, his cell phone held to his ear. Despite the giggles and general air of fun, she had good control of her bunch. True, there were only seven of them, but at least they were routinely connecting with the ball and each other. He was less certain about the little jig she had them doing at the end. Then he realized that Ellie herself was dancing with the ball, dribbling in place. She let the kids try, none with success, but they were keen to work at it, and that, he had to admit, was half the battle.

As the practice wound down, cars began arriving with parents picking up their children. Asher made one more phone call, this one to his sister Petra in Waco, who just needed an opportunity to vent. The things she saw, working the night shift at an upscale Waco hotel, made her question her career choice, but as she was in the final semester of earning her degree, he, of course, counseled her to stick with it. She had known that he would; she just needed to hear someone say it.

With their brother Phillip basically unreachable and Dallas unsympathetic, Petra had no one else to whom she could turn. Their parents would only tell her that she should have opted for med school. Asher suspected that they were hurt because none of their offspring had followed in their footsteps. They were wonderful Christian people and good parents, but they lived and breathed medicine to the point that little else existed for them. That attitude had prejudiced their children against medicine as a career.

He finished his call and looked around. Ellie sat sideways on a rough bench, her cell phone in her hand. Asher wondered where her ride was, but he waited until everyone else had gone before approaching her.

"Kent running late?"

"Yeah, he's stuck in traffic. He had to run into Dallas to pick up a drug for some sick kid, and you know how that traffic is, especially at this time of day."

"Doesn't he have his own car?"

"He does, but it's been in the shop. Again. I'm sure it's ready to be picked up by now."

"Kind of like you."

She laughed, but he noticed that she had yet to look at him. "I thought about asking Ilene for a ride, but she already had a car full of kids. She really wants this team to make it, you know, so her daughter can play. She's recruited half the kids herself, and I have to say they're pretty enthusiastic. There will be a lot of disappointed kiddos if we're shut down."

Asher said nothing to that. She seemed to be implying that he should bend the rules, but he couldn't. Nevertheless, he felt a bit like an ogre.

She seemed uncomfortable now that everyone else had gone, and he couldn't really blame her. Their private meetings never seemed to go very well, but he couldn't drive away and leave her there on her own, so he sat down on the bench. For a long moment, neither of them spoke. Finally, he took it upon himself to make conversation.

"Can I ask you some—"

"Ask away. I've got nothing to hide."

He knew that was a reference to the fire and his grilling her that day in his office, but he didn't want to go there, not now.

"Sorry," she muttered. "Didn't mean to interrupt."

"I was just wondering why you didn't play soccer in college. You obviously know your way around the game."

She shrugged. "I only wanted to go to BCBC, but so did nearly everyone else on my team, and some of them were better soccer players than me. Besides, I had other options."

"Such as?"

"An academic scholarship. Couple of grants." He was impressed. After a brief pause, she spoke again in a wistful voice. "When you don't have parents willing to take responsibility for you, you can sometimes get a little extra help."

He was sorry he'd asked. Despite their dedication to medicine, his parents had never shirked the smallest responsibility, especially not when it came to their children. He'd attended one of the best universities in the country, and even though they'd been disappointed in his field of study, they'd paid every nickel that his soccer scholarship hadn't covered. He'd been that rare graduate who hadn't owed a penny in loans, and his siblings had followed in his footsteps. Maybe it was time that he stopped resenting his parents for wishing he'd become a doctor.

"Can I ask *you* a question?" she said after a moment.

He quailed at the thought, but he'd started this. "Okay."

"I've been thinking about something Dallas said a long time ago. She said that the law was your second choice. It's none of my business, but I can't help wondering what she meant by that."

He crossed his legs at the ankles. "She meant that I wanted to play professional soccer."

Ellie swiveled around on the bench. "Really? Why didn't you?"

"Blew out my knee in the middle of my junior year," he said, rubbing the scar that ran alongside his kneecap. "They yanked my scholarship when the rehab didn't go well."

"That stinks."

"The team gave me another shot my senior year, but I knew I wasn't going to get picked up, so I enrolled in—"

"How could you know that?" she interrupted, and this time he found himself smiling at the interruption.

"I just did. I prayed about it, and deep down I knew that God was telling me to give up my dream."

"That can't be!"

"We all eventually give up our dreams, Ellie. It's part of growing up."

"I don't believe that. The way I see it, if God doesn't change your heart's desire then He just brings it to you in another way or at another time. Look at David in the Old Testament. In his youth, he obviously aspired to music and poetry, but God called him to be king. And yet we have the Psalms as proof that David realized his dream of composing music and praise lyrics."

"We also have Job as an example," Asher pointed out. "He said it himself. 'My days have passed, my plans are shattered, and so are the desires of my heart.'"

"Yes, but God gave it all back to him. He even doubled Job's wealth because Job remained faithful and sought righteousness."

"You're thinking of your grandfather now, aren't you?" Asher said, his tone sounding accusatory even to his own ears.

"I am, and why not? He's a good man, a godly man, and he's waited patiently and faithfully for what he wants."

"And you're not above 'helping' God to see that he gets it, are—"

"Yes!" she erupted, launching onto her feet. "I admit it. I tried to stall the insurance settlement so Grandpa could have time with Odelia, but I see now that was a lack of faith on *my* part. My faith doesn't figure into it, though. It's Grandpa's faith that counts, his and Odelia's."

Asher felt a surprising urge to tell her what Odelia had revealed the night before, but he decided not to get involved. It was not his grand scheme. He looked at Ellie and felt a momentary rush of warmth for her, this woman who believed so strongly in romantic love.

"Come on. I'll drive you home," he said, getting to his feet.

She folded her arms mulishly, but she followed him to the SUV. While they drove toward Chatam House, she called her grandfather to tell him not to come to the soccer field, then gave him a glowing report of her first practice. The SUV swung through the gate and tooled up the hill. Asher brought it to a stop right in front of the walkway.

"Hilda probably has dinner ready. I'm sure your aunts would be happy to have you at their table again," she said.

He shook his head even though she was perfectly correct about his generous aunties. He just didn't think he could sit across a table from Ellie tonight—he needed some recovery time, so to speak. "Best get on. Give my love to my aunties for me."

"I will," Ellie promised, sliding down to the ground. "Thanks for the ride."

Nodding, he drove away, knowing that skipping dinner was a pointless gesture. He was already thinking about when he was going to see her again.

What could God possibly be doing? Was He allowing Asher to be beset by unfathomable events meant to test faith and resolve? Or was He making a point that this lowly attorney could not seem to grasp?

As he watched Ellie disappear into the house, he had a feeling it was the latter.

"My sister's husband was a brutal man," Hilda said, tucking a thick stack of paper napkins into the basket that she had filled with three dozen plump, fragrant ginger muffins still warm from the oven. She had insisted on providing them when Ellie had mentioned wanting to pick up some ready-made variety for the meeting at Asher's house. "I feared he'd kill her before she could get away from him," Hilda confessed bluntly, "but the Misses called Mr. Ash, and he took care of it."

A large woman with thin, straight, gray hair cropped bluntly just below her ears, Hilda ruled the kitchen at Chatam House with a stern but indulgent hand. Covering the basket with a crisp, white cloth, she pushed it across the chrome worktable toward Ellie, saying, "It's the least I can do after Mr. Ash handled Carol's divorce free of charge." That, apparently, had been years ago, and Carol had since joined the staff at Chatam House as a maid.

Ellie thanked Hilda and carried the basket out to her truck, belting it into the passenger seat. She couldn't help smiling at this new information about Asher. Apparently, he'd always been willing to help anyone his aunties brought to him. She wondered if that was the limit of his largesse and somehow doubted that it was. He volunteered as youth soccer commissioner, after all, and that had to be a big job. She felt a certain pride in that, even though she knew she had no right to such pride.

Everything told her that she had zero chance with Asher Chatam. Even this beautiful, modern home made that clear. It was the exact opposite of the aging, modest Victorian house that she so loved. Asher was serious and confident; she preferred a sunnier outlook but constantly doubted herself. He projected a maturity far beyond his years; she still often felt like a mercurial teen. He was successful and ambitious; she loved teaching and had no plans beyond that.

She had to face facts. As much as she admired Asher, she wasn't cut out for a man like him. So why would God put her in the way of a broken heart like this—unless it was for Asher's sake? Perhaps her purpose was to help Asher see the possibilities, even if she herself was not intended to be his. Well, so be it—she'd do what she could.

Squaring her shoulders, she pressed the doorbell and stepped back, grasping the handle of the basket with both hands. While she waited, she glanced around at the tall, arching entryway. Built of creamy white stone, it contrasted nicely with the rough brown brick and mossy green trim. She was not so admiring of the landscaping. Even with the arched drive crowded with vehicles, the plantings seemed rigid and unnatural. Ellie couldn't help musing that Asher could use the assistance and expertise of his Aunt Magnolia and her gardener.

The door opened abruptly, signaling the impatience of her greeter. Asher stood there in faded jeans with a simple sweater over a plain white T-shirt, the sleeves pushed up to expose strong forearms lightly sprinkled with cinnamon-brown hair. Ellie couldn't help but smile.

"You're late," he barked.

Ellie's smile abruptly faded. "I am not. It's four minutes 'til nine."

"Everyone else got here ten minutes ago."

"Good morning to you, too, Asher. I brought

some muffins," she said, wondering what she'd done to deserve such a greeting.

He glanced at the basket then turned and waved, indicating that she should follow.

Ellie stepped across the threshold.

A raised dining area at the rear of a sunken living room hosted a long, rectangular table and armless, tan leather side chairs. A wall of glass looked out over a stone-rimmed swimming pool and several wood benches flanked by empty planter boxes. At least a dozen people, mostly men, sat or stood around the table. Nearly all held stiff paper cups of coffee. Each was dressed casually in some type of athletic clothing. And every one of them stared at her as she stood there in black flats, black leggings and an electric blue, long-sleeve tunic.

Ellie knew instantly that she had overdressed. Without even realizing it, she had dressed to impress. She had instinctively dressed for Asher without a single thought to who else might be in the room—or the actual purpose of the meeting. Her face heated.

Asher walked to the table and pulled out an empty chair before continuing on to another space at the far end.

"This is Ellen Monroe, team two-sixteen."

"There are two hundred and sixteen teams?" Ellie asked, surprised at the large number.

"Uh, that's sixteen teams in tier two," a man explained. "We're all tier two here today."

Ellie nodded to the group and set the basket on the table just as someone else said, "I didn't know that team made it."

"It hasn't," Asher announced, pushing around some papers on the table. "They have a coach now but not the minimum number of players."

"Yet," Ellie said with a smile.

At the same time, the buff, fortyish man next to Ellie commented pointedly that "something" smelled good. A tall, slender woman with long, light brown hair reached across the table and lifted the corner of the crisp white cloth covering the basket.

"Muffins. Mmm."

"From the cook at Chatam House," Ellie confirmed, removing the cloth. "Help yourselves."

A muscle flexed in Asher's jaw as everyone surged toward the basket. Several minutes filled with happy chatter and appreciative noises as the assembled company enjoyed Hilda's muffins— everyone but Asher, who stood at the end of the table with his arms folded, watching Ellie with an expression she couldn't read. Reminding herself that she had done nothing wrong, she sat and nibbled at her own delicious treat while someone farther down the table poured coffee from an insulated carafe into a paper cup and passed it to her. After her second sip, Asher called the meeting back to order.

The group immediately quieted. Asher began speaking, noting alternate schedules, outstanding fee payments, issued equipment, even team colors. Ellie learned that her own team had been assigned the color yellow and that Ilene Riddle had turned in all the necessary funds, with the exception of Ellie's own fifteen-dollar payment for her coach's jersey.

"I'll have to get it from my car later," she said, realizing only belatedly that she'd interrupted him. He didn't so much as glance in Ellie's direction before picking up where he'd left off in midsentence.

Ellie mentally bit her tongue. Obviously, Asher Chatam was a harsh taskmaster. His volunteer coaches came ten minutes early for meetings and sat in silence as he spoke. More proof that she did not fit his model of acceptability. A few moments later, she realized that everyone was staring at her.

"What?"

Asher pinched the bridge of his nose and spoke, obviously repeating himself: "In the event that your team makes it before the deadline, you'll need to decide on a team name."

Thinking of yellow-and-black team uniforms, she almost said, "Bumblebees," but at the last moment, she realized that probably wouldn't sound fierce enough. "Yellow Jackets," she offered.

Asher nodded curtly. "Now, the scheduling. Since we have a questionable team, I've had to draw up two schedules for this tier. The first requires each team to play two games in one day at some point during the season. The other..."

Ellie listened intently, hearing some muted grumbles as Asher laid out the entire scheme. The brown-haired woman leaned forward and spoke to Ellie out of the corner of her mouth, "Übercompetitive."

"They're six- and seven-year-olds, for pity's sake," Ellie muttered back. "How competitive can they be?"

"Not the team, the coach."

"Ah."

"Any questions?" Asher asked, looking directly at Ellie.

Embarrassed and irritated, Ellie snapped, "Yes, as a matter of fact, I do have a question. Since we're playing 'small-sided,' I don't understand why I have to field a minimum of nine players."

"It's true we only field five players on each side at this age, but you must have substitutes," one of the other coaches pointed out.

"And you hardly ever get all the kids there at one time," someone else put in.

Ellie shrugged. "If enough kids don't show up to play, you forfeit the game."

"It's the rule," Asher said flatly, obviously intending to close the subject.

But Ellie wasn't ready to let it go, and why should she? It wasn't as if giving in would change anything. "Why should seven kids not get to play for lack of two?" she asked.

"Let's not take up everyone else's time discussing it right now. Anything else?" he asked, looking at the others.

Ellie leaned back in her chair, folded her arms and fumed until the meeting ended a few minutes later.

As everyone else filed out, Asher parked one hip on the edge of the table and helped himself to a muffin.

"There are reasons for rules, Ellie," he said quietly, "and we all have to follow them."

"You don't have to tell me that. I'm a kindergarten teacher. But what about fun? Soccer's a game. Games are supposed to be fun."

He shook his head. "I can't make an exception, Ellie, no matter how much I might want to. The other coaches would be all over me. Surely you can see that."

She decided to try another tack. "You've obviously forgotten how important having a little fun is."

"I have lots of fun," he said, looking slightly startled.

"Oh, yeah? Name one fun thing that you do."

He shrugged. "Being soccer commissioner is fun for me."

She rolled her eyes. "So you enjoy long hours, meetings and laying down the law."

"Okay, I admit, that part's more about the kids, but I like soccer. I watch it on TV all the time, and I make every live game that I can. Besides, I'm not just the commissioner. I'm a referee, too, and I even coach."

"It's a proven fact that kids learn best when they're having fun. Now, if you want to see some real fun and how it impacts learning, just drop by my classroom sometime. I'll be glad to demonstrate."

He looked directly at her. "I don't have time for that."

"Well, you'll be at church tomorrow, won't you? I teach a pre-K class. Stop by during the Sunday School hour. We have a blast, and the kids learn plenty."

"I have to finalize upper-tier schedules tomorrow. I usually leave after the early service, anyway."

They stared at each for a long moment. Then

Ellie conceded, swallowing back further comment. Obviously, he was letting her know that he intended to keep her at arm's length. She told herself that it was better this way.

Okay, Lord, she prayed silently. *Lesson number one. Don't push.*

Ellie began removing the remaining four or five muffins from the basket. "Hilda said you were to get any leftovers."

Asher nodded. "Thank her for me."

"I will. Think about coming by tomorrow. Everyone could use a little reminder of what real fun is from time to time, including you, Asher."

Papers in one hand, basket in the other, she turned and hurried toward the front door.

Chapter Eight

Sunday morning found Odelia unaccountably depressed. Stepping down into the foyer, Odelia walked slowly across the marble floor toward the front parlor, tugging at the white cuffs on the long sleeves of her navy blue dress. She'd bought this garment years ago for a funeral, but in the end she hadn't been able to bring herself to wear it. The thing was just too severe and depressing. Today, however, it somehow seemed appropriate, as did the small pearl earrings and simple gold chain that she had chosen for accessories. She usually went for much more gay attire, but this morning she'd looked at her colorful closet and collection of fun jewelry, and absolutely everything had felt wrong. Only this suited her current mood, and it would certainly do for church.

She meandered into the parlor to find Hypatia standing next to her customary wingback chair, a frown on her face as she stared down at the settee, where Kent Monroe sat with a cup and saucer balanced on one knee.

"Don't trouble yourself," Kent was saying. "I really don't need the sugar in my diet, anyway, and I wouldn't want to make you late for Sunday services."

"No, no, it will only take a minute," Hypatia replied. "My sisters haven't even come down yet." She tapped her cleft chin with the tip of one finger. "I just can't remember the last time that Hilda forgot the sugar bowl." She dropped her hand. "Well, no matter."

She turned, saw Odelia and did a mild double take before exclaiming, "Odelia, how fine you look! Very elegant." She moved toward the door, patting Odelia's shoulder as she passed. "Excuse me for one moment. Hilda has forgotten the sugar bowl."

Odelia stood uncertainly in the center of the floor, torn between fleeing the room and allowing herself just a few moments of Kent's company. The latter desire won out over the self-protective impulse, and she walked, head down, to the armless side chair at one end of the occasional table.

"May I pour you some tea?" Kent asked solicitously.

"Oh. No. Thank you. I'm not in the mood just now."

Kent's cup and saucer clattered as he set them back on the tray. He slid across the settee to the corner nearest her and leaned forward, speaking in a soft voice. "My dear, I'm concerned by your subdued manner. This isn't like you."

Forcing a smile, Odelia said, "It's just the end-of-winter doldrums. You know how it is. The promise of sunshine one minute, gray skies the next, and the thermometer can't make up its mind whether it's on the way up or down."

"Well," Kent said in a dubious tone, "I look forward to your spring magnificence, then. I must say, I miss your more colorful self."

Delight brought roses to Odelia's cheeks. The next moment, dismay leeched it away. Clearing her throat, she changed the subject.

"Have you found your cat? I know you were looking for it again yesterday."

Kent sighed. "I suppose I shouldn't be concerned. He's just a stray tom, and you know how they are, but I guess I got used to seeing him around. He certainly kept the vermin out of the garage. I just can't help wondering where he is now. The fire must have traumatized the poor old thing."

"I could organize a search if it would make you feel better," Odelia offered automatically.

Smiling, Kent reached over and squeezed

her hand. "I've always admired that huge heart of yours."

Odelia gasped. "How can you say that? You, of all people!"

He seemed surprised. "Odelia," he said quietly, "I've always understood why you refused to go through with it."

"You have?"

"Absolutely. Triplets share an unusual bond. I know why you can't leave your sisters to live with me."

"But you were so wounded at the time."

"Well, of course, I was! The beautiful girl who had stolen my heart was not going to be mine. I admit I was bitterly disappointed, but even then I understood why it had to be that way."

She shook her head. "I—I don't know what to say."

"You don't have to say anything," he told her kindly. "And you're still that beautiful girl who stole my heart."

She laughed stiltedly at that, telling herself that he was just being his usual charming self. He couldn't help it really. She'd always loved that about him. Correction. She had always *appreciated* his natural charm.

Closing her eyes at the lie, she sent up a silent prayer. *Father God, help me overcome these foolish feelings. I know it's too late for romantic love,*

*especially as nothing has changed. Even if Kent
could care for me again, how could I possibly
leave my sisters now? Forgive me for not being
properly grateful for the life that You've given me
and the many blessings that I've known. Amen.*

She felt a little better afterward. Whatever was
she doing, anyway? Eating her heart out at her
age. Ridiculous!

Ridiculous and so very depressing.

"Something is definitely wrong with Odelia,"
Kent observed softly as Ellie slid behind the
wheel of her truck.

Glancing over at him, she shifted in order to
straighten the slim skirt of her cherry-red dress.
He sat slumped down in the passenger seat, cran-
ing his head to watch the long, storm-gray town
car carrying the Chatam sisters turn out of the
drive and onto the street. Anxious not to be late
for Sunday school, Ellie quickly buckled her seat
belt, started up the engine and engaged the trans-
mission.

"What makes you say that, Grandpa?"

He sat up a little straighter as the truck moved
forward on the gravel drive. "She's wearing navy
blue."

"Navy blue what?"

He shrugged. "Just…navy blue. A dress, I

guess. Nothing spectacular. I'm not sure she's even wearing earrings."

That did sound serious. Ellie could not remember a time when she had seen Odelia Chatam without big, wild earrings.

"This is all my fault," Kent growled.

"How is it your fault?" Ellie asked, glancing at him worriedly.

"She was fine before I moved into Chatam House," he rumbled.

"You don't know what she was like day-to-day before we came to Chatam House," Ellie pointed out.

"I sense that she is disturbed!" Kent argued, shaking his hands in frustration. "I feel it!"

"Why don't you talk to her about it?"

"I've tried."

"Try again."

He rubbed a thick, heavy hand over his face. "I don't know. If my presence is upsetting her—"

"Pray about it first, then."

"I pray about it every day," he murmured. "I pray for her every day. I have for the majority of my life."

That was so sweet that Ellie blinked back tears as she drove toward the Downtown Bible Church. She felt a great yearning for worship today. She hadn't felt such need to be in God's house in a very long time. Perhaps because deep down she knew that she would have to accept disappointment for her grandfather as well as herself.

They spoke no more as she parked the truck at the curb in front of the pharmacy and they got out to walk around the square to the stately old church. A few steps later, Kent headed off to a senior men's class, and Ellie hurried to the children's wing.

"Sorry I'm late," she called as she reached the prekindergarten play space.

Her coteachers, Sherry Hansen and Anna Burdett Chatam, who was married to Asher's cousin Reeves, paused while laying out supplies in the craft area to greet her with smiles.

"No problem," Sherry said. "We've still got a few minutes."

Ellie pulled the appropriate posters and props from the cabinet mounted on the wall and prepared the scene while bantering with Sherry and Anna, the latter of whom was well known for her wit. Anna's stepdaughter, Gilli, kept up a steady stream of chatter as she helped distribute cotton balls.

The other children began to arrive, in ones and twos at first, then in flurries of a half dozen or more, until some forty-plus were climbing over the large, plastic play gym or sitting down to tables to create pastoral scenes with cotton balls, cutouts and glue. Ellie sat down in the middle of the gym set and allowed the children gathered there to climb over and around her as they played.

At the proper time, she gathered them up and herded them to the story station. Taking her place on a small, low chair, with the children arranged in a semicircle on the floor around her, Ellie guided the children through a short prayer. When she looked up again, she saw Asher standing outside the hallway. He had an oddly wistful look on his face and a little half smile.

Ellie's heart clunked. When she'd invited him to stop by this morning, she'd just been trying to make a point about how children learn best through fun. She hadn't really thought that he would take her up on the invitation. Indeed, he'd indicated that he would not. Now she wondered how long he had been standing there and why he had come. She couldn't quite believe that he meant to take instruction from her. At any rate, she didn't have time to deal with him now, as the child tugging on her skirt reminded her.

"Miss Ellie? Miss Ellie!"

She dropped a quick smile on the impatient boy, but when she glanced back to the window, Asher had gone.

* * *

"All aboard the Homebound Train! Woo-woo!"

For the second time in three days, Asher watched Ellie in action, this time through her classroom door. Hopping around to present her back to the class, she pretended to pull the string of a horn then crouched slightly and moved her bent arms in a churning motion.

"Chugga-chugga-chugga, chugga-chugga-chugga. Remember your tickets! How do you get your tickets?"

"Put away your stuff!" a child called.

"And get your backpack!" someone else yelled.

One by one, children tucked away their toys and art projects and ran to grab their backpacks from hooks on the wall. Laughing and giggling, they fell in behind her and clamped their hands onto the shoulders of the person ahead.

"Chugga-chugga-chugga. Here we go!"

She's right, Asher thought, watching her rock back and forth as she pretended to build up enough steam to pull away from the station. *I really don't know much about fun.*

He'd watched her two days earlier in the Sunday School classroom when she'd all but become a part of the indoor gym set. She'd looked so happy, and the kids all obviously adored her. He'd felt a strange pang, wondering if he had ever been that happy. His work certainly didn't lend itself to her kind of gaiety, and he couldn't remember now when soccer or anything else had really been fun for him.

He didn't know what had compelled him to stop by her Sunday School classroom that day; he hadn't even intended to go to church last Sunday, but somehow he couldn't stay home. Then, after the early service, when he usually slipped out, he'd found himself walking the maze of halls until he'd come to the pre-K unit. He didn't know what he'd expected to see, but he couldn't seem to help himself. Not then. Not now.

A call to the school on Monday morning had told him that he could not gain access to Ellie's background check without her. He could have asked the school staff to have the form signed, but instead he'd said he would take care of it himself. Now here he stood on a Tuesday afternoon, watching her at work and wishing he hadn't been quite so hard on her lately.

Happily *chug*ging, the line of children followed Ellie on a snaking trail through the room, winding in and out of low tables and miniature chairs, finally coming to a stop at the door. An electronic bell sounded just then, and utter chaos erupted. Up and down the hall, doors flew open, spilling children and teachers out in a noisy rush. Inside Ellie's room, however, the children waited patiently, smiles on their faces, while she traded places with her assistant.

Asher backed up as Ellie swung open the door and stepped out, facing away from him. "Bye. See you tomorrow. Have a good evening, everyone."

Ellie's class followed the assistant down the center of the hall and through the chaos to an outside door, beyond which waited parents and buses. Asher started forward to make himself known, only to jerk back again as several older children dashed past him and through the door into Ellie's classroom.

"Hold on!" she called, laughing. "I haven't booted it up yet. Give me a sec."

Leaving the doorway, she walked across the room to a computer station. Asher, as yet unnoticed, followed.

"Hurry, hurry," one little girl urged. "My mom will be here any minute."

"You can go first to show Donnie how it's done," Ellie said, as music swelled from the computer. "But then you have to let him play."

"It's a soccer game," Asher said, unaware that he'd spoken aloud until Ellie whirled to face him.

She smoothed the surprise from her face, backing up a step. "Yes, it is. This particular game is designed to teach the rules of the game."

"Really?"

"It gives you a scenario and several options for how to play it. Choose correctly and your play succeeds. Choose the wrong option and your opponent, in this case the computer, gets the ball, but only after the computer shows you the correct play. You go on until someone gets a goal scenario. Choose correctly then and you score."

"That's marvelous," Asher said. And fun, obviously.

A cry of jubilation went up from the kids gathered around the computer.

"You didn't come here to watch computer games," Ellie said to him.

"I did not," he acknowledged, presenting the form in his hand. "I need your permission in order to get a copy of your background check for the league records."

"No problem." She took the paper from him and carried it to her desk, where she picked up a pen and signed her name.

Meanwhile, a little boy at the computer was hitting buttons with lightning speed. Suddenly, everyone cheered, and the boy began to jump up and down.

"I won! I won!"

"And very quickly, too," Ellie praised. Moving forward, she bent at the waist to bring her face level with his and asked, "So what do you think? Would you like to play real soccer?"

"Uh-huh, yes! I wanna play!"

Reaching back, Ellie whipped a sheet of paper off her desk and presented it to him with a flourish. "Take this to your parents. If they have any questions, they can call me."

"Okay." Clutching his paper, the boy turned back to the computer, where another child was taking a turn.

"An effective recruiting tool, too." Asher smiled.

"It certainly is." Picking up some papers from her desk, she handed them to Asher.

He glanced over them, his eyebrows rising. "You've already signed up three new players. You've made your team in a single day."

Ilene Riddle stuck her head in the door just then. "Let's go, kids. I'm double-parked." Three of the children trooped to the door, protesting as they went. "You, too, Donnie, your mom's waiting outside. Ellie, Commissioner, see you tomorrow."

"See you!" Ellie called as the group disappeared. The boy raced after the others, waving his enlistment form.

Asher shook his head. "You never cease to amaze me."

She smiled and said, "I'll take that as a compliment. Thank you."

"You're welcome."

"Wanna play? The upper levels are pretty challenging."

"Oh, no," he said, shaking his head. "I shouldn't."

"I dare you."

"No, really, I should—"

"Coward," she said with such a daredevil grin that he couldn't quite manage to be offended. "I'll go easy on you, I promise."

He was surprised by how much he wanted to play that silly game with her. And why not? What would it hurt?

He shrugged out of his coat. "Now I'm going have to beat you at your own game. Literally."

"Ha!"

He pulled up two chairs while she plugged in the controllers and programmed the game. All those toggles and buttons were confusing at first, but before long he was giving her a challenge. It became evident quickly that they were fairly evenly matched, but Asher wasn't about to push his luck, so the moment that he tied up the game, he called it.

"I could beat you if I had time, but I'll settle for a tie in the interest of my schedule."

"In your dreams, bub. I admit that I probably couldn't keep up with you on a real field but—"

"Probably?" he scoffed playfully.

"But I've got this sewed up," she bragged, grinning. "I was going easy on you, remember?"

"Now who's dreaming?"

"Hang around and find out."

"Wish I could," he said, "but I have to change and get to the soccer field." He hauled himself to his feet and turned to see a tall, thin, familiar young man wearing a wrinkled shirt and a frown in the doorway.

"Ellie," the man said abruptly, "we need to talk."

Behind Asher, Ellie groaned. "Not now, Lance."

Ignoring her, he stepped forward and put his hand out to Asher, introducing himself. "Lance Ripley. We didn't meet last time."

Asher slid into his coat, avoiding shaking hands with the man, whom he disliked instinctively, having witnessed him lay his hands on Ellie over a week ago. "Asher Chatam."

The fellow flushed, his ears turning red. Abruptly, he switched his attention back to Ellie. "It's been too long since we went out. We'll have dinner together tonight."

"Uh, no," Ellie said flatly.

Smiling to himself, Asher glanced over his

shoulder. As he'd expected, she'd folded her arms. He almost wished she hadn't. That was *his* pose, the one he so often elicited from her. Lance Ripley had no right to it. Or to her, no matter what he thought.

"Now, Ellie," Lance said, "you know you don't mean that."

"Lance, I am *not* going out with you again."

"We'll have a nice dinner and talk this over," he said reasonably.

"No. We won't."

"I'm afraid I can't accept that."

"I'm afraid you have no choice," said Asher, unable to stay quiet any longer.

Hostile, ice-blue eyes swung his way. "I don't see what you have to say about it."

"Oh, I have quite a lot to say about it, actually. I'm Miss Monroe's attorney, the one who will be filing the restraining order if you don't leave her alone."

Watching the tumblers fall into place in Lance's mind, Asher felt a greater sense of satisfaction than he had known in some time.

"You're *that* Chatam."

"Indeed I am. And you are not welcome. Remember that the next time you approach my client. She doesn't want to see you, not here, not on the street, not at Chatam House. I trust I've made our position clear."

Eyes wild, Lance Ripley glared at Asher, his mouth working silently around unspoken words. Then he blinked, visibly calming himself, and lifted his chin before spinning away and disappearing.

Asher smiled, only to feel a hand snatch angrily at his elbow and turn him about. "What are you doing? He's going to think I'm suing him for harassment!"

"Maybe you should. He has harassed you, hasn't he?" Asher was puzzled by her anger.

"That depends on your definition of harassment."

"Mine happens to be the legal one," Asher told her. "I'd like to hear yours."

Sighing, she dropped down onto the corner of her desk. "Okay. Maybe he has been a bit persistent."

"Well, I don't imagine he'll be coming around here anymore."

"Oh, yes, he will," she retorted. "That's the problem. He works here. I can't help running into him from time to time."

Asher literally gnashed his teeth over the thought. "I'll speak to him again."

"No!"

"You told him no. That should be the end of it."

"I just told you no, too."

He ignored that, another thought occurring. "I still can't believe you went out with that jerk on Valentine's Day."

"No one wants to sit home alone on the most romantic night of the year."

Asher had, for a long time. He'd proposed to Samantha on Valentine's Day, and he'd spent every one alone since they'd divorced. That seemed pointless now, a silly excuse to ignore the "most romantic night of the year," as Ellie put it. Apparently, she hadn't found this past Valentine's Day date quite so romantic, though.

"Look, Ellie, are you sure that you haven't rebuffed some other guy who might have taken it out on your house?" he asked roughly, trying to get his mind off Valentine's Day.

She shook her head, laughing in a forlorn way. "Look, I'm just not the sort to inspire that kind of passion."

"Oh, yes, you are," he replied. Ellie's jaw dropped. Scurrying to recover, he babbled, "I—I mean, according to the insurance company, *someone* set that fire. If not one of your, ah, disappointed boyfriends, then who?"

She looked positively stricken. Coming to her feet, she glanced around as if looking for threats in the shadows, her full lower lip clamped firmly between her teeth. Asher realized suddenly that she was trembling. Because of him. Because he had frightened her with his rash words.

"It's all right," he promised, stepping forward to take her into his arms. "You're safe. No one's going to hurt you. I promise."

She nodded, resting against him. "I know."

"I mean it," he told her, tightening his hold. He couldn't help noticing that she fit neatly into his arms. He barely had to lift his chin to accommodate the top of her head. "Don't be afraid. I'll take care of everything."

"H-how can you?"

"I'll just do my job."

She shook her head, asking softly, "So, the insurance company thinks the fire was intentionally set?"

"They've implied as much. So I don't want you or your grandfather talking to anyone about the fire without me there. Understand?"

Gulping, she nodded and turned her face into the hollow of his shoulder. Somehow, his hand found its way into her silky, springy hair.

"If anyone contacts you, refer them to me," he instructed softly. "No interviews unless I okay them."

"All right," she said huskily. "Thank you." She tilted her head back, her lovely violet eyes holding his. "You were right about me not being in favor of you handling this."

"No. Really?" he quipped with a lopsided grin.

"But I'm really glad now that you are."

"Me, too," he said. It seemed appropriate to cup her face in his hands then. Until he realized he was about to kiss her!

Mentally recoiling, he derailed himself in time to land the kiss in the middle of her forehead, as if she were a child.

She stepped back, her head bowed. His hands drifted down to his sides. She cleared her throat and turned away. "Will I see you at practice tomorrow?"

He jammed his hands into his coat pockets. "Um, maybe. Probably not. I don't know," he stammered, confusion clouding his mind.

"Okay," she said lightly.

He pretended to check his watch, saying, "Gotta run." He managed a single step.

"Ash."

The sound of her speaking his name stopped him right in his tracks. Cautiously, he turned back and saw that she held out the signed form.

"Oh. Right." Slipping forward, he gingerly took it from her. "Thanks."

She sent him away with a single nod.

He couldn't wait to get out of there. And at the very same time, he could hardly bear to go.

Which was reason enough to run for his life.

Chapter Nine

It didn't take a sledgehammer to penetrate her thick skull—a brotherly kiss to the forehead managed that just fine. That kiss in her classroom yesterday had made it abundantly clear that Asher was not attracted to her, no matter what her runaway imagination wanted to say about it. Oh, she had thought for a moment that he had meant to give her another kind of kiss entirely, but reality could not be denied. She simply did not draw men like him. No, she attracted the kooks and goofballs.

Ellie turned away from the parking area where Asher, dressed in a black warm-up suit, was exiting his SUV. He had been so ambivalent about being at practice today that she had not expected to see him here, and for once she wished that he had stayed away. Looking down at herself, she sighed. This had seemed like such a fun, clever idea last night, but she could just imagine how Asher would see it. Too late to worry about that now. Determined to make the best of it, she put on a smile and ran toward her gaping team, her arms full of yellow tulle and caps. The wings on her head flapped and the tutu that she wore over her athletic gear fluttered as she moved.

Dredging up as much enthusiasm as she could, Ellie passed out the tutus to the girls, who slipped them on over their workout shorts as instructed, giggling uncertainly. The boys got bright yellow caps decorated with black felt wings like hers. Partially stiffened, the wings flapped as the wearer's head moved. Once the laughing kids had donned their respective costuming, Ellie broke out the black cotton gloves. She'd sewn the fingertips of both hands together to remind the children not to use their hands.

"Okay, let's line up for drills." She demonstrated the proper technique of handling the ball, showing them how still her tutu and wings remained when she did it right.

The kids worked at it uncertainly at first but with increasing progress as the practice went on. Ellie was aware that the other teams on the field had stopped to gawk. She even heard one little girl run to her mother and whine, "I wanna soccer tutu!" Ellie smiled. Not only were her players the envy of their counterparts, they were developing greater dexterity and finer technique, too.

Blowing her whistle, Ellie signaled the start of a scrimmage. She rotated a different kid into the net every few minutes, reasoning that they all needed to know what they were up against on both sides of the ball. Before long, they were all pretending to be goalies making heroic saves. Ellie called them back to their purpose by reminding them that goalies did not score goals. She then pulled aside her best two goalie prospects and told them that goalies helped win games by keeping the other team from scoring. She rotated those two in and out of the goal while allowing the other kids to take one-on-one kicks before starting a new scrimmage.

By the end of the practice, Ellie could feel that the team was coming together, and she had almost forgotten that Asher was watching from the sidelines. Almost, but not quite.

Deciding that the tutus and winged caps had served their twin purpose, she took back only the gloves before removing her own "learning aids" and turning to face Asher. The kids ran to grab juice boxes and pretzels from Ilene before racing off to their respective parents, tutus fluttering and wings flying.

Asher stood with his hands clasped behind his

back. Determined to take her medicine without flinching, she walked over to him, tutu and cap in hand.

"Your technique is stellar. Your methods, though…" He shook his head.

She folded her arms, and his lips twitched. Then an instant later, he burst out laughing in great, wrenching guffaws. Sighing, she waited out his attack of hilarity, waving from time to time as players or their parents called out farewells.

"Sorry," he gasped. "Can't help it. Never seen…such a thing…in my life!"

She tapped a toe impatiently while he got himself under control. "It worked, didn't it?"

Wiping his eyes with both hands, he nodded. "Quite possibly. They're certainly the most enthusiastic team in the league, I'll give you that. But you understand that they have to play in regulation uniforms."

"Of course I understand that they have to play in regulation uniforms," she retorted, glancing at her cleats. "They don't have to *practice* in regulation uniforms, though, do they?"

Asher shook his head, still grinning. "There's no rule about practice gear," he began, "so long as they wear knee and elbow guards and rubber cleats, but—"

"It's just a bit of fun," she argued, "and they're learning. You saw that for yourself."

"Fun, again." He shook his head in disbelief. "Yeah, okay, fine. It's your team. I'm not going to interfere."

Relieved, Ellie pressed her hands together in an attitude of prayer. "Thank you. That's wonderful, because I have an idea about—"

He raised a hand, palm out. "Don't tell me! I don't want to know."

"Why not?"

"Because," he said, "there is a principle known as plausible deniability." He gave her a lopsided grin. "And the way things are going, sweetheart, I have a feeling I'm going to need it."

Throwing up his hands, he turned and walked back to his vehicle, chuckling and muttering that he'd be lucky if he wasn't asked to resign his position. She dismissed that concern immediately. What she could not dismiss—what she would think about time and time again—was that he had called her *sweetheart*.

Still grinning and shaking his head, Asher drove away. The sight of Ellie in a tutu and winged cap had made his eyes water with laughter. What amazed him, however, was the way her tutued and cap-winged team had caught on to her technique. The woman had a true gift for teaching kids, as well as a talent for making life bright and—he had to admit it—fun. More fun than he'd had in eons.

She also had a way of banishing his good sense. So why was it, he wondered, that he couldn't manage to keep away from her?

Even if she wasn't his client, she was still too young, too naive, too…*exuberant.* And the only commonality he could point to, really, was a mutual regard for family. Okay, so they both liked soccer, but her approach couldn't have been more different than his. It was like comparing Roman gladiators to Keystone Kops.

They were both Christians, too, of course, but her "brand" of Christianity seemed to be a kind of feel-good, pie-in-the-sky, God-is-going-to-take-care-of-everything hope, while his was… He had to think about that. His interpretation of Christianity was responsibility and righteousness, he decided, endurance, sober self-knowledge and acceptance of certain facts without complaint. This, after all, was not Heaven, he reminded himself, so naturally it lacked…what? Happiness?

Verses from the fifth chapter of Galatians ran through his mind.

But the fruit of the Spirit is love, joy, peace, patience, kindness, goodness, faithfulness, gentleness and self-control.

Frowning, he examined that list of qualities.

He had love, lots of it, the love of God and the love of family and friends. He could do without the romantic kind, which was why—he congratulated himself on this—he had peace. Although sometimes it actually felt as if he had too much peace, but then perhaps he was equating peace.

Patience he had in abundance. Mostly. About most things. He tried to be kind and others were, often enough, kind to him. Goodness brought to mind the aunties, which made him smile. As for faithfulness, no one, absolutely no one, could say that he was not faithful. Gentleness? Well, when it was called for, he supposed. And self-control was something upon which he prided himself.

Did that, he wondered, make it a sin instead of a blessing? He frankly didn't know.

That left only…joy. Which was not, Asher reminded himself, the same as happiness, though he had both. Didn't he?

Certainly, he enjoyed many things. But that was not the same, was it?

How, he wondered, could he enjoy so much in his life and yet not know for sure if he had joy? Had he missed something? He thought of Ellie, who had essentially lost both of her parents and was now effectively homeless, with no assurance that she would ever regain what she had lost. Yet, somehow, he sensed that she knew a kind of joy that he lacked. Maybe his "theology" was wrong or incomplete.

Good grief, she had him doubting his core beliefs. Why was it, then, that he couldn't seem to hold her in anything but the highest esteem?

That question remained in the forefront of his mind as he arrived at the high school athletic field. The schools were good about sharing assets with the Buffalo Creek Youth Soccer League because so many of their middle and high school players came up through the system. He wondered if they'd be quite so cooperative, however, if the coaches and athletic directors ever got a load of a certain BCYSL coach's teaching technique.

After parking the truck, he grabbed his black cap and cleats from the passenger seat. Skirting the home stands, he threw his legs over a rail to reach the grass. Several teenage boys were already involved in a scrum. Two more came loping across the field from another direction. One of them, Rob Holloway, was a fairly new recruit. He had lots of promise. Try as he might, though, Asher couldn't seem to get the switch to flip inside that kid's head.

An image of Ellie dribbling and booting the ball in her tutu and floppy-winged cap flickered in Asher's mind. His hand went automatically to the yellow flags he had in his pocket, and an idea was born. Or rather, reborn, since it was Ellie's to begin with.

He tore a flag into four somewhat equal sections, pinning one to the top of his cap with a safety pin from the stash he kept to repair the nets. He left the ends to drape down on either side of his ears. Gesturing to Rob, who wore a hooded sweatshirt, and two other boys who had caps, Asher took out his cell phone and handed it to one of the more trustworthy kids with instructions to film what was about to happen.

He helped the boys pin on the floppy cloths, then appropriated the ball and led them out onto the field to start a vigorous short-sided scrimmage. One of the boys comically tossed his head as if the scrap of fabric were actually a mane of luxurious hair. After a few minutes of play, Asher called a halt and had the boys follow him to the sideline, where he reclaimed his phone and took a look at the video.

"Here," he said, tapping the tiny screen. "And here. Do you see what I'm talking about, Rob?"

"My head's all over the place!" the boy exclaimed, watching his yellow cloth flop and flutter while the others remained somewhat stable.

"That's what I mean by 'core discipline,'" Asher explained, enjoying seeing the light go on in Rob's mind.

He heard a lot of laughter on the field that day, and a good deal of it was his own. As they left the field at the end of practice and called out their farewells, they no longer addressed him as "Mr. Chatam." He was "Coach" now. Maybe for the first time.

And he knew exactly whom he had to thank for that.

"I don't suppose my granddaughter has put in an appearance yet?"

Odelia looked past Hypatia to find Kent standing in the doorway. He looked tired. In Odelia's opinion, he ought not to be working at all. Yes, he went in to the pharmacy late and came home early, limiting himself to four days per week, but at his age he should have been enjoying a life of leisure and looking after his health, not counting pills and mixing syrups. He certainly shouldn't have been dealing with house fires and insurance companies, which was why Asher had been called in.

"As we've just told Dallas, we haven't seen Ellie this evening," Magnolia told Kent, passing a cup of tea to their niece, who occupied the gold-striped wingchair.

Dallas had practically become a fixture at Chatam House since the Monroes had moved in. Odelia appreciated the frequent visits, though probably not for the same reasons as her sisters. She loved having family around, of course, just as they did, but these days she appreciated the distraction even more. Despite her best efforts, her gaze wandered back to Kent, who openly stared at her.

"What a lovely ensemble, a harbinger of the bright spring days ahead."

Knowing that her mood had affected her appearance, Odelia had made a concerted effort to punch up her appearance that morning, choosing a grass-green skirt and flowered blouse, along with a headband sporting a pink daisy and yellow daisy-chain earrings that hung almost to her shoulders. Kent noticed, even if no one else seemed to have done so.

Her cheeks heating with ridiculous pleasure, Odelia thanked him while pretending a great interest in the hem of her full skirt. What a goose she was to let a simple, polite comment set her heart racing!

After a moment, Kent excused himself and went upstairs, remarking that he needed a nap before dinner. Odelia let herself relax a bit, only to note a wry, knowing smile curling one corner of her niece's lips. Dallas sipped her tea and ate a cinnamon cookie, obviously biding her time.

Blessedly, before she could comment on Kent's compliment, Ellie came in.

"Sorry I'm late. It was an eventful practice." She crossed the room, wearing shorts with knee socks and a vibrant yellow T-shirt, the only portion of her outfit that Odelia could truly approve. The yellow cap was fun, too, though. Its black wings flopped forward and back, like a pair of clapping hands, as Ellie collapsed onto the chair before the fireplace. "I am so out of shape!"

"Interesting hat," Dallas remarked, amber eyes dancing.

Ellie groaned and swept the thing off, leaving her curly hair in disarray. "Teaching aid," she explained tersely, tucking it beneath her.

"Oh?" Hypatia said brightly. "What subject, dear?"

"Soccer, Miss H. Didn't I say? I'm coaching a soccer team for six- and seven-year-olds now."

Dallas plunked down her cup and saucer, jostling the other contents of the tray. "Get out of here! You never mentioned that."

Ellie grimaced. "Didn't I? It came up unexpectedly not long ago."

"Puh-leze," Dallas drawled. Grinning at her aunts, Dallas added meaningfully, "And I suppose the fact that Ash is the soccer commissioner has nothing to do with anything."

Odelia immediately brightened at that reminder. Trading looks with Magnolia, she smiled. "So he is. Well, well. I had forgotten all about that."

Hypatia lifted her eyebrows, and Odelia knew that the sisters were all thinking the same thing: whenever anyone came to stay at Chatam House, a romance inevitably followed. But Ellie and Asher?

"Who'd have thought it?" Odelia chirped happily, distracted for the moment from her own problems.

"Who'd have thought what?" Ellie asked.

Hypatia shrugged. "I suppose it was inevitable."

"What was inevitable?"

"That a romance would be brewing," Magnolia declared jovially.

Smiling over the rim of her cup, Dallas leaned back into the corner of the armchair and crossed her long, slender legs.

Ellie glanced at Odelia, smiling slightly. "O-kaay. And the 'brewing romance' that we are discussing is…"

"Why, yours, dear," Odelia answered brightly.

"Mine?" Ellie yelped, sitting forward. "Whatever gave you the idea that I'm having a romance?"

"Oh, just the facts," Dallas said nonchalantly.

"First, you were alone out in the greenhouse with Ash the other evening—"

"*You* arranged that!"

"So? I was told by someone who would know that it was a lengthy tryst."

Ellie glanced from Dallas to Odelia and back. "Who would that be?"

"Garrett Willows, as it happens." She slid a look at Odelia from beneath her lashes, adding, "In fact, I heard there was quite a bit of traffic in the greenhouse that night."

Odelia felt hot spots blossom high on her cheekbones. They had been spotted, she and Kent! Oh, no, no. It couldn't be.

"I don't care what you heard," Ellie said emphatically. "There was no 'tryst,' as you put it." Odelia allowed herself the tiniest bit of relief.

"No?" Dallas scoffed. "And I suppose it's just a coincidence that you've now gone from client to coach in my brother's soccer association?"

"Yes! That's exactly what it is, a coincidence."

"Oh, my dear," Hypatia said with an indulgent shake of her head. "There are no coincidences for God's children."

"It's a concept young people seem not to grasp anymore," Magnolia said, tsking.

"Wow," Dallas exclaimed, sitting up straight as if an idea had struck her. "A twofer."

Odelia blinked at that, horrified. "A what?"

"A twofer. You know, it means two for the price of one."

"I'm sorry, dear. I don't understand," Hypatia said.

"If there are no coincidences," Dallas explained, "then it can't be a coincidence that Mr. Monroe is in residence here at Chatam House, either."

Hypatia shrugged in confusion, while Odelia's face flamed hot. "I suppose."

"Well, then," Dallas went on, nodding at Odelia as if encouraging her to confess all.

Odelia felt the color drain from her face. "Y-you can't possibly mean…"

Dallas glanced around the gathering. "Oh, come now," she said with some exasperation. "Ellie isn't the only Monroe staying here."

"What does that have to do with anything?" Hypatia demanded.

"All I'm saying is that if Ash can fall in love, anyone can, even…" She looked pointedly to Odelia.

Gasping—squeaking, really—Odelia lurched to her feet. Only belatedly, as she was juggling them, did she realize that she still held her teacup and saucer. Somehow, she managed to get them safely onto the tray, but by that time, everyone was gaping at her.

"Excuse me," she said, lifting her chin. "I have to…"

The thought trailed off. She couldn't think of a single thing that she had to do just then. Except escape. Which was exactly what she did. She quite literally turned tail and ran, and she didn't stop until she was locked safely in her room in the suite that she shared with her sisters.

Whatever could Dallas be thinking? she wondered, wringing her hands as she paced the floor. Obviously, Garrett had seen Kent follow her to the greenhouse that night, or perhaps Asher had mentioned something about their discussion afterward. No, no, she couldn't accept that. Ash was the soul of discretion. Yet, what Dallas had said could not be entirely dismissed.

"No coincidence," she muttered. "No coincidence."

But no romance, either.

Not for her.

Not for a foolish old lady who had missed her chance long ago.

Chapter Ten

Glancing at her sister's rapidly retreating back, Magnolia frowned at her niece. "Whatever has gotten into you, Dallas Chatam?"

"Surely you've noticed—" Dallas began, only to break off at the sound of the door knocker.

"Who might that be?" Hypatia murmured, casting a curious look over one shoulder.

"Whoever it is," Magnolia said, setting aside her teacup with a huff, "you'll have to entertain without me. I don't have time for any more nonsense today. Spring will not wait for my repotting." Casting a frown at Dallas, she rose and hurried away, leaving Hypatia to reluctantly answer the door.

Ellie seized the moment to hiss at her friend. "I agree with Magnolia. What is wrong with you?"

"Just stating the obvious," Dallas retorted defensively.

"The obvious, my foot! Making them believe there's something between your brother and me."

"Well, isn't there?"

"No! Besides," Ellie went on, realizing that she ought not to dwell on the subject of her own nonexistent romance, "you practically had Odelia in tears."

"Oh, please," Dallas protested in a harsh whisper. "Auntie Od in tears? I may have embarrassed her a little, but—"

"A little? You think that was *a little* embarrassing? Sometimes I think you're certifiably insane."

"That's harsh," Dallas muttered with a frown.

"Not harsh enough," Ellie scolded hotly, "not if you—" She broke off as Hypatia reentered the room. Hypatia, however, was not alone.

Behind her strode an attractive, boyish-looking fellow with neatly groomed nut-brown hair. Dressed in a dark blue button-up shirt with a somehow familiar logo embroidered in white above the breast pocket, he smiled benignly, his sharp gaze tracking from Dallas to Ellie and back again. Not much taller than Hypatia, he carried a simple dark blue folder in his left hand. In other words, he seemed utterly harmless—until Hypatia pointedly said, "Ellie, dear, this gentleman would like to speak to you and your grandfather."

Ellie stared hard at that logo and gulped. "I…h-he…"

"I've explained that Mr. Monroe is taking a much-needed nap," Hypatia went on helpfully.

At that point, the fellow dodged around Hypatia and went straight to Ellie, putting out his right hand. "Jared Lawrence, Miss Monroe, with Insurance Nation."

"In-insurance. I see."

He seemed unconcerned when she failed to immediately take his hand. "I have some questions about the fire at 1001 Charter. But first…" He plucked a sheet of paper from the folder. "I'll need you to sign this interview document. It's just to fix the time and date of our conversation and attest to the validity of your stateme—"

"Y-you've caught me at an in-inconvenient moment," Ellie interrupted, sliding sideways out of her chair. "Please excuse me." Her gaze followed his as he looked down at the crushed, winged cap that she had left behind on the seat of her chair. "While I change," she improvised quickly, snatching up the thing and tucking it beneath one arm.

With a sharp nod, she bolted for the door. Behind her, she heard Hypatia stiltedly offer Jared Lawrence a cup of tea. Ellie didn't catch his reply as she hurried across the foyer to the gear bag that she'd left on the floor. Dropping down onto her haunches, she reached into the bag for her cell phone before darting up the stairs.

By the time she'd made the turn in the broad, sweeping staircase, she'd located Asher's phone number and hit Send. She hurried into the small apartment that the Chatam sisters referred to as the East Suite. Seeing that her grandfather's bedroom door was closed, she crossed the sitting room to stand before the fireplace.

"Answer. Answer," she pleaded as the phone rang on the other end.

Just when she thought all hope was lost, she heard a click, then a cautious, "Hello, Ellie."

She didn't bother with a greeting, just blurted, "You said not to talk to anyone unless you were here, but he's downstairs in the parlor right now!"

"Who?"

"Jared Lawrence. From Insurance Nation. He wants me to sign a paper and talk to him."

"Sign nothing, say nothing," Asher instructed sternly. "I'll be right there."

He ended the call before he could hear her say, "Thank God!"

Glancing gratefully toward her grandfather's closed door, she hurried toward her own bedroom at the opposite end of the suite. Without waiting for the water to heat, she quickly rinsed off beneath a cold shower, managing to keep her head mostly dry in the process, then changed into jeans and a sweater. After stepping barefoot into leather clogs, she dragged a brush through her unruly hair and headed back downstairs. Asher was shaking hands with Lawrence when she reached the parlor.

"I believe we spoke on the phone not long ago," Asher said, looking as if he, too, had just stepped out of a shower, his chestnut-and-champagne hair plastered sleekly to his head.

"I believe we did," Lawrence confirmed genially.

"And I thought it was understood that I would serve as point of contact for the Monroes," Asher went on.

"Ah," was the noncommittal reply.

"I don't appreciate the end run," Asher stated flatly.

Jared Lawrence just smiled. "Noted." Taking an ink pen from his shirt pocket, he flipped open the folder in his hand and asked, "So when and where exactly would you like me to conduct the interviews?"

Obviously, this man was not going to be put off indefinitely. Ellie chewed her lip and caught Asher's eye as he glanced in her direction.

"Perhaps," Asher said slowly, "it would best serve everyone's purpose if the interviews were to take place at the Monroe house."

Jared Lawrence nodded his agreement. "Very well. Visuals are always appreciated."

"I'll arrange to have the house opened and let you know when we can meet."

Lawrence closed his folder and pocketed his pen, saying, "I look forward to hearing from you soon." Lawrence smiled at Ellie. "Give my best to your grandfather when he wakes."

"Yes. Thank you," she returned softly.

Nodding deeply to Hypatia, he said, "I appreciate the hospitality."

"Our pleasure," Hypatia murmured.

Dallas, who had observed all in silence, rose then. "I'll see you out."

Still smiling, Lawrence followed her from the room.

Ellie immediately crossed to her customary chair and collapsed upon it with a gusty sigh.

"Not so fast, my girl," Asher said, pulling her up by the arm again. "I'd like a word with you in private."

"Use the library, why don't you, dear?" Hypatia suggested, sounding weary.

"Excellent idea," Asher said, striding off in that direction with Ellie in tow. Dallas turned from the door just as they crossed the foyer. Her eyes widened, a speculative gleam lighting them.

Ellie groaned, but Asher did not slow down until he'd closed the library door behind them.

"We are out of time," he stated flatly. "I need straight answers."

Ellie glanced away. "I've given you straight answers." To those questions he had asked, anyway.

"Do not be fooled by that man's mild manner! He may be young and all smiles, but he knows exactly what he's doing, and today's little stunt tells me that he's clever. Beyond that, if I were a betting man, I'd lay odds that he knows something that I do not. So spill it, Ellie!"

"Spill what?"

"You're holding something back."

She threw up her hands. "I've given you the facts exactly as I know them!"

He stared at her for several moments, one hand moving agitatedly against his thigh until he clapped it to the back of his neck. "Something is missing from this picture, and if you can't supply it, then I need to speak to your grandfather." He looked up suddenly. "Is your grandfather having financial difficulties?"

"No! We may not be wealthy, but the Monroes have always been solvent. I don't make much money, of course, and I do have student loans, but to my knowledge, Grandpa has no major debts."

"What about a mortgage?"

"The house was inherited. I don't think it has

ever carried a mortgage. The drugstore is free and clear and brings in a steady income."

"How were you paying for the renovations?"

Ellie shrugged. "Grandpa said there was money. I suppose it has to do with the drugstore. He took in a young partner a few years ago and recently struck a deal to sell. Not immediately, but over time. I assume there was a substantial down payment, and there had to be savings, too. Of course, it's all gone now. Grandpa paid off the contractor after the fire."

"That may have been a mistake," Asher mused. "It's possible the contractor or subcontractor was negligent."

Sighing, Ellie felt tears well up. It was all such a mess. She was tired and hungry and overwhelmed with worries about Dallas and Odelia and, especially just then, her grandfather. She had tried so hard to take the burden from him and protect Dallas in the process, but nothing was going as she'd hoped. The more immediate concern, however, was one she'd pushed to the back of her mind.

"We're never going to get back into our house, are we? But where are we going to go?"

"Hey," Asher said, "it's not like you're going to be out on the street."

"But we can't stay here indefinitely, and if we can't get the house back into shape…" She sniffed and tried to swallow back the lump thickening in her throat, but she could not keep the tears from falling. "G-Grandpa should be r-retiring and t-taking it easy, but I don't know if that will be p-possible now."

Asher patted her shoulder awkwardly. "Don't cry. That won't help."

"D-don't you understand? I can't p-pay rent for the two of us, but it's not fair for him to have to c-continue to work. He deserves better than this!"

Against his better judgment, Asher reached out and pulled her into his arms. "It's going to be okay."

She sniffed and closed her eyes, her head upon his shoulder. "You don't know that."

"I promise you." Pushing her away a little, he framed her face with his hands, tilting it upward. "Just work with me, sweetheart. We can't be at odds here. We have to be a team. Okay?"

"Okay," she echoed, smiling softly as she gazed into his amber eyes. "A team."

"That's my girl," he said, and then he set his lips to hers.

It was a completely natural gesture, a light, comforting kiss, but it quite literally curled Ellie's toes.

Suddenly, Asher wrenched away, leaping back so far that he bumped up against the door. Her hand lifted to her lips in wonder. He abruptly spun about, wrenched open the door and strode through it without a word.

Ellie ran forward, intending to call him back, but before she could get out a word, Dallas appeared. Ellie jerked to the side to look over her friend's shoulder, only to see Asher pulling the front door closed behind him. Deflated, she glowered at her friend.

Squealing like a teenager, Dallas grabbed Ellie by the shoulders and walked her backward into the room. "He called you 'sweetheart'! I heard it!"

"You were eavesdropping," Ellie accused.

"Duh. Did he kiss you? It sounded to me like he kissed you."

Oh, he had kissed her, and it hadn't been a brotherly affair this time, either. Ellie felt a smile tugging at her lips, but the memory of what had followed changed everything. That kiss had been an accident. Obviously, he hadn't intended to do it. There had been nothing romantic about it, not on Asher's end, anyway. He'd simply meant to comfort her and gotten carried away.

The thought brought fresh tears to her eyes. Suddenly, she couldn't help feeling that Dallas was very likely responsible for the train wreck that her life had become. If not for that fire, she'd never have been thrown into Asher's path. She'd never have let her girlish crush burgeon into something so desperate, and her grandfather and Odelia wouldn't be tiptoeing around the house like scalded cats. No matter how lofty Dallas's motives might have been, Ellie just could not feel in charity with her best friend at that moment.

"I am not listening to your nonsense, Dallas Chatam, not now. I'm facing a major problem here, in case you've forgotten."

In typical fashion, Dallas waved that away with the flop of her wrist. "Ash will take care of that."

"He's not a magician, Dallas. I have no doubt that he'll do what he can, but even he can't predict what the insurance company will do."

"Oh, come on. They'll pay. Besides," she said, waggling her eyebrows, "I'm less interested in how Ash is handling the insurance company than how he's handling you."

"Stop it!" Ellie hissed. "You don't know what you're talking about."

"So tell me."

"There is nothing *to* tell. And I don't want to talk about it anymore."

Huffing, Dallas parked her hands at her waist. "Well, that's no fun. You always tell me everything."

"What part of *nothing* do you not get?"

Dallas rolled her eyes. "Fine. So let's talk about your grandfather and my aunt Odelia."

Ellie wasn't much in the mood for their usual confab, but she parked herself on the edge of the large, rectangular table in the center of the floor. "I'm not sure there's anything to discuss there, either."

"Are you kidding? After the way she behaved earlier? No, I'm telling you, this is working. Getting them together under the same roof is the smartest thing we've ever done."

"We?" Ellie shook her head. "This wasn't my idea, Dallas. I'd never have thought of moving in here."

"Too true," Dallas admitted. Winking, she added, "I take every bit of credit for that particular stroke of genius." She reached around and patted herself on the back, grinning widely. "I cannot wait to tell my know-it-all big brother that I was right about Odelia and Kent!" With that, she whirled away and made for the door, saying, "Gotta run. I have a PTA meeting tonight. We'll talk more later." She paused to wag a finger at Ellie, adding, "And don't think you can spare the details indefinitely just because he's my brother."

She all but skipped through the door, leaving Ellie to wonder glumly just how far her friend would go to achieve her ends—and just how much longer she could go without asking Dallas for the truth.

Wincing at the slam of the door behind him, Asher paused on the deep porch of Chatam House. The guilt he'd been trying to outrun slammed into him, dealing a full body blow that made him stagger and moan.

He had done it. Good grief, he had actually kissed her! He hadn't just thought about it. He hadn't just anticipated it. He'd actually done it.

Dear Lord, what's wrong with me? he mentally howled, but before he could pursue that prayer to any satisfactory conclusion, a familiar voice called to him.

"Asher? Dear boy, whatever is the matter?"

He spun on one heel to find Odelia sitting in the same position where he'd last seen her, except this time she was swathed from head to knee in white faux fur. She appeared, in fact, to be wearing a hooded cape, which on anyone else would have been an oddity.

"Is something wrong?" Odelia pressed, obviously alarmed by his silence.

"Uh. No. That is, there was an insurance investigator here, and I was called in to run a little interference."

"Oh. I didn't realize. I only saw your car pull up

in front of the house from my bedroom window, but by the time I made my way down here to wait for you, there was no one else about."

"He didn't stay long," Asher said, moving on to the more salient point. "You wanted to see me?"

Odelia smiled, but her gaze remained troubled. "Oddly enough, you seem to be the only one I can talk to about my situation."

Asher was almost relieved, and the irony of that was not lost on him. Just days ago he'd rather have taken a blow to the head than talk about his old auntie's crush on a past beau. Now, it seemed a much-needed distraction from his own tortured feelings. He would not think of *that* as a crush. No, no, a mature man did not form a crush on a woman young enough to be his…okay, daughter was a stretch. Still, she was too young.

Shaking his head, he walked over and took a seat next to his aunt. "How can I help you, Aunt Odelia?"

"I'm not sure you can, dear," she admitted, looking down at her lap. "I'm not sure anyone can. It's just that I'm so confused."

"About what exactly?"

She bit her lip, her capped teeth making significant indentations in the thick layer of bright pink lipstick that she wore. The sight made Asher smile despite everything. It struck him suddenly that despite the fact they'd been born on the same day, Odelia had somehow managed to stay younger than her sisters. He hadn't realized it before because their looks, if not their styles, were so similar. Something vibrant shone from Odelia's countenance, something that made her seem strangely innocent.

"Do you think it's possible," she finally began, "to find love at my age? Romantic love, I mean?"

No sprang to the tip of his tongue. It was the wisest answer he could give her, the surest. But he couldn't say it. He looked at that sweet face and those sad, yet expectant eyes, and he couldn't find the strength to crush her dreams.

"There is much to consider for someone in your position," he began carefully, only to feel the words he wanted to say dwindle away. Several awkward moments passed, during which he felt uncharacteristically unsure of himself. Gulping, he finally said, "I have to answer with a qualified yes. Anything's possible, after all..." He paused again, struck by the hope that had kindled in her eyes. Realizing suddenly that he couldn't argue his way out of this with logic alone, he stopped trying and gave her what she obviously needed to hear. "Yes. I think it's possible for someone your age to find love and romance."

She stared off into the distance. "Well," she

said finally, "it's a moot point. Even if Kent should harbor some true feeling for me after all this time, nothing has changed. I still can't contemplate leaving my sisters, you know, not that I would expect to have the opportunity, mind you." She shook her head. "No. Regardless of what Dallas says, it's not my romance that God has ordained this time."

"This time?" He tilted his head, feeling that he'd missed something important.

She reached across and patted his knee. "I'm so very glad for you," Odelia told him warmly.

He had definitely missed something important. "I don't understand."

"Now, don't be coy. We've come to expect it, you know."

"Expect what?"

Odelia giggled. "Surely you've noticed. Every time someone seeks sanctuary in this house, a romance soon follows. Yours is no exception."

"Mine!" he yelped, jerking sideways in his chair.

"Well, yours and Ellie's. Tell me," she went on curiously, "when did you first notice her that way?"

Notice her? Notice Ellie? *That way?*

The truth blindsided him, knocking him out of his chair and onto his feet.

He had noticed Ellie the first moment that he'd

laid eyes on her, when she'd been nothing more than another incoming freshman at BCBC. He'd instinctively buried the attraction beneath the knowledge that she was his baby sister's friend and, therefore, too young and off-limits. She was *still* too young.

Wasn't she?

Client, he reminded himself desperately. Baby sister's best friend. Fifteen years his junior. Client. Plus, he had no intention of ever remarrying. He did not want to get married again. Period. End of discussion.

Apparently not, however, so far as his aunt was concerned.

"I wouldn't have put you and Ellie together," Odelia was musing, tapping the cleft in her chin, "but God always knows best about these things."

Asher searched for the words that would lay to rest her romantic expectations on his behalf once and for all. "I fear you've misconstrued the situation, Aunt Odelia. Ellie is not…my type." Unless not being able to stop thinking about her said otherwise.

"No?"

"I mean, she's a delightful wo…er, girl." He couldn't quite remember when he'd started thinking of her as a woman.

"Such a sunny nature," Odelia confirmed with

a smile, "and you know what they say about opposites attracting. Oh, not that you're dour by any means, just so very…serious," she finished apologetically.

Asher stared at her for a full five seconds, no idea what to do or say. In the end, he took the coward's way out. Shivering, he clapped his arms about himself. "Brr. Chilly out here. Easy to forget it's still technically winter until the sun sets, isn't it?" He got up and sidled toward the steps at the edge of the porch, babbling, "But you didn't forget, did you? Nice and toasty in that lovely cape, I imagine. Me, I am…" *The world's greatest idiot.* "In a hurry. Sorry." He darted forward and smacked a kiss on her cheek then rushed to the steps, calling, "Stay warm. See you later."

"Bye-bye, dear," Odelia returned, lifting a hand in a tentative wave.

Asher fled as if someone had set the hounds on him. It was not, he reflected later, his finest moment, but it paled in comparison to what he'd done there in the library with Ellie, and it did not haunt his dreams that night.

Ah, no.

When at last he turned out the lamp on his bedside table that night, he dreamed, not of flight, but of kisses and violet eyes that seemed to look straight into his shabby soul.

Chapter Eleven

"The house is Ellie's inheritance," Kent Monroe said, laying an arm on the edge of Asher's desk as he leaned forward in earnestness. "It's all I have to leave her, you see. My young partner at the pharmacy is making semiannual payments on the buy-in, but upon my death, everything having to do with the business goes to him."

Asher nodded. It was standard practice for partnerships, particularly if one of the partners carried a heavier load in conducting the business, as Asher assumed Monroe's younger partner did. Certainly the man had made no complaint when Asher had stepped into the pharmacy Friday morning to ask Kent for a word in the privacy of his office down the street.

"So the renovations were in aid of assuring the integrity of your granddaughter's inheritance," he said, intentionally suggesting a valid argument in support of their case.

"Just so," Mr. Monroe confirmed.

"And you paid for those renovations with the funds from the buy-in?" Asher asked hopefully.

Monroe shifted back in his chair, letting his hands fall onto his knees. "Not entirely. I had other funds."

"Savings."

"Some." Monroe sighed. "It's all gone now, of course, with very little to show for it, I'm afraid. Oh, the upstairs was not damaged by the fire, so technically what I paid for remains, with minimal smoke and water damage, but what difference does it make with the downstairs unlivable? I suppose I should be thankful that it wasn't the renovated portion that burned."

Asher tapped a finger against the arm of his chair, considering. Kent's version of events dovetailed neatly with Ellie's, and yet he could not escape the feeling that something was amiss.

"Can you think of anything else that I should know about this matter?" he asked.

Kent Monroe shook his balding head, but Asher noted that he averted his gaze. "Of course, I'm no lawyer."

Asher studied the man for a moment longer, trying to see him as Odelia and Ellie did, but his lawyer's sense told him that like his granddaughter, the old fellow was not being entirely forthcoming. Stymied, Asher decided not to press the matter further—for the moment.

"All right. Thank you for your time, Mr. Monroe."

Looking greatly relieved, the older man said, "Kent, please."

Asher rose to his feet. "Well, then, Kent, I'll see you on Monday afternoon at three-thirty."

Kent took several seconds to hoist his bulk to a standing position, but his handshake was strong when he grasped Asher's hand in farewell. "Oh, ah, Ellie says a quarter of four is about the best she can do. Something about bus duty."

Asher sighed. Ellie hadn't been out of his head for ten minutes at a stretch in the past forty-eight hours. Just the mention of her name drove him to distraction, and he couldn't afford to be distracted—not with the insurance adjuster about to return to the scene.

After seeing Kent out, Asher returned to his desk, but his disquiet would not yield to the usual panacea of work, and he eventually turned away from the computer screen to pray.

"Lord," he whispered, "I don't know what I ought to do now, but all I ask is that You please somehow help me protect Ellie."

Only after the words had left his mouth did he realize exactly what he'd said or what it was that weighed so heavily upon his heart. It was no surprise, really, that he hadn't recognized it earlier. In his lifetime, Asher rarely had known real fear. Bitter disappointment, yes. Heartbreak, even. Loss. Failure. Shame, too, once or twice... the entire gamut of negative human emotion.

But this was the first time he'd felt such fear for someone who had become so important to him.

On the following Monday afternoon, Ellie turned the truck into the familiar narrow drive and got out to walk around to the front, where she huddled inside her hooded raincoat, waiting for her grandfather to join her. Asher stood on the front porch of the house, his luxury SUV at the curb. The day had taken on a gray cast and sputtered intermittently with a cold, brittle mist that would have coated the ground with a slick sheet of ice only a couple weeks earlier. Today, it produced only gloom, which seemed sadly appropriate.

Dreading what was to come, Ellie surveyed the beloved old Victorian house. As always, its white, pink and pale gray gingerbread exterior, complete with a turret, elaborate trim, shutters and tall brick chimneys, evoked thoughts of horse-drawn carriages and courtly manners, of young girls in wide-skirted ball gowns and prosperous gentlemen in swallowtail coats. However, it no longer quite felt like home.

How odd. She still felt very much a guest at Chatam House, and this place had always been home to her, even when she'd lived elsewhere with her parents. Yet, that somehow seemed in the past to her now.

Asher walked down the three broad, wooden steps to the cobblestone walkway that bisected the shallow front yard and stood impatiently, his hands brushing back the sides of his suit jacket to lightly bracket his waist. Ellie hung back enough to let her grandfather take the lead. He traded words of greeting with the younger man and trudged up the steps. Asher met her gaze grimly before holding out an arm in welcome or perhaps encouragement. She walked ahead of him up the steps and into the deeper gloom of the porch, wishing she could have a moment to speak to him. But now was not the time.

The X-shaped metal bar that the fire department had bolted across the front door had been removed and now lay to one side. Without preamble, her grandfather opened the door and went inside. Ellie followed, the scent of burnt wood and fabrics assailing her nose.

Gray streaked the flocked green-and-white wallpaper in the entry; brown water stains mottled it into a garish mess. The red oak hardwood floor had been scorched in a wavy pattern right up to the edge of the narrow staircase with its delicate, hand-turned spindles. Soot covered everything, including the small but elaborate chandelier overhead.

Down the hall, she could see the remains of the kitchen with its warped cabinets and soggy, molding linens. Only the tin ceiling panels had kept the ceiling from falling down in that room. They had not been so fortunate in other parts of the house.

Turning left, they took in the parlor. It looked like nothing so much as a garbage heap. The heavy velvet curtains had burned right to the rods, one of which had fallen down. Chunks of ceiling plaster hung down like spooky, ragged flags and covered what sodden furniture still existed in great gray clumps and fine white spatters. The carpet had melted to what was left of the floor, and the far wall had burned to the studs.

The only truly intact section of the room was the fireplace, which shared a sturdy brick wall with the dining room. The brick and mortar would need a great deal of scrubbing, but at least the ornately carved wooden mantle remained untouched.

After looking around for a few minutes, Asher nodded at a burned-out section of the parlor floor where the couch had stood. "Is that where it started?"

Some oblong lumps of charcoal were all that was left of the sofa, which had sat facing the doorway, and the tall, narrow table that had stood behind it. A rusty-looking tin can, a small, twisted rod and a few shattered pieces of milky, grayish glass showed where the lamp had fallen.

Her grandfather nodded. "Yes, that's it. The lamp stood on a table at the back of the couch, and the workmen had placed some tools and supplies behind there so they'd be out of sight. It was a tall lamp on a tall, narrow table. Gave good light, that lamp."

There were no overhead lights in the parlor, and the large glass shade on that lamp had provided ample illumination, which was why they'd kept it despite its top-heavy proportions. Ellie suspected that her grandmother had added the wide, domed, cobalt blue glass shade herself years earlier.

They talked through what information they'd been given and their own actions of that day several times before the insurance company rep arrived. To their surprise, before he asked a single question, he walked them through what he knew, and by the time he was done, it had become abundantly clear to Ellie and everyone else that the paint remover had been turned over *before* the lamp had fallen.

"I just assumed that the lamp had to fall and knock over the can," her grandfather said, shaking his head. "The lamp was top-heavy, after all, and the plastic bucket with the paint thinner inside was on the floor."

Lawrence made a noncommittal sound at that and walked over to the window. "The other window on this wall has a storm unit affixed to the outside. This one does not. Why?"

"Cross ventilation," Ellie supplied. "My grandmother hated the central air unit after it was installed and often preferred to open a window, but she had a difficult time with the storm windows, which is why we removed one on each side of the house for her. We just never replaced them."

"But it was cold that night, wasn't it?"

"Yes."

"So why open the window?"

"Paint fumes," her grandfather answered. "The house reeked of them, and since we were busy moving things around, we were warm enough."

"I notice that it has no screen," Lawrence pointed out.

Kent grimaced. "I put a hoe handle through it while raking leaves last fall. I wasn't in any hurry to fix it. No insects in winter even if the window does have to be opened."

Again, Lawrence made that noise, which was beginning to sound skeptical to Ellie. "So you left the house open while you moved furniture into storage?"

"Not intentionally," Ellie told him. "I meant to close the window before we left." Actually, she'd thought she had, but she'd opened and closed that window so many times since the renovations had started that she couldn't remember one instance from another.

"Don't suppose it would have mattered," Lawrence said lightly, "since the fire department reported that they'd found the front door unlocked when they arrived."

Ellie's jaw dropped. At the same time, an expression of horror came over Kent's face.

"That…that was my fault." He looked to Ellie apologetically. "I know I said I'd take care of it, but when you mentioned locking the front door, that reminded me that I needed to look up the code to open the storage unit. Once I'd done that, well, I forgot about the front door."

"Then anyone could have come into the house after you'd left," Asher quickly pointed out. "Isn't that right?"

Ellie gulped and nodded worriedly. "I suppose." Anyone could have—but Dallas had been the one on the scene. Which was the last thing she wanted to point out to Asher.

Lawrence just smiled and asked who might have had reason to set the fire. Who, he meant, besides the owners of the house. Ellie said nothing. All her words and thoughts from that point on were reserved for God.

Asher had to give the young investigator credit for not blustering and pressing for answers. Then again, it was to the insurance company's benefit to delay making a ruling on the case. By denying the claim without overwhelming evidence of wrongdoing on the part of their insured, they opened themselves up to a lawsuit. On the other hand, they could delay settlement via patient investigation. They had some very reasonable questions, after all. The problem was that in at least a couple of instances, the Monroes had no reasonable answers.

When he returned to the house after seeing Mr. Lawrence off, he found Ellie perched on the porch swing.

"Grandpa's looking around out back for his cat," she said, sliding to make room for Asher. Feeling unaccountably weary, he sat down. A number of issues clamored for attention, but he couldn't seem to organize his thoughts just then. The gray of the day mirrored his gloomy mood perfectly.

"Think you'll have to cancel soccer practice?" Ellie asked.

"Already have."

"What about tomorrow?" she asked.

He shrugged. "We'll have to see."

Nodding, she used her feet to put the swing in motion, pushing against the floor of the porch. Asher let himself settle back and enjoy the lulling sway of the hard bench seat beneath him. Seconds later, however, he realized that he had to say something. He locked his knees, halting the movement of the swing.

"Ellie, I apologize for the other day. That kiss never should have happened."

She made a small sound of distress, but when he looked at her, her gaze was trained woodenly on her lap.

He plodded on doggedly. "I don't usually do that sort of thing. Especially not with clients. Especially not with young clients who could misunderstand how these things can—"

She got up and leaned a shoulder against a slender post supporting the porch roof, her back to him. "I'm not stupid, you know."

"I never thought you were."

Putting her spine to the post, she folded her arms and glanced at him before dropping her gaze to the floor. "Your aunts and sister think we're having a romance."

"I know." Asher sighed and leaned forward to

prop his elbows against his knees. "But they're wrong," he added softly.

"Are they, Asher?" she asked. Not waiting for an answer, she sent him an unreadable look then pushed away from the post, turned and calmly walked down the steps, putting her hood up. He watched her go to her truck and slide in behind the steering wheel. An instant later, she started up the engine. After a few moments, Kent trudged around the house and got in.

Asher sat where he was until the little truck had backed out and gone on its way. Finally, he pulled out his phone and called the fire department, asking for someone to come and put up the door blocks again.

Asher sat behind his desk and stared at the computer screen, trying to bully his mind into co-operation. He had a case coming up on the local docket and needed to prepare, but he couldn't focus. The gray weather seemed disinclined to lighten, spitting chilly rain for another day. He'd had to call off soccer practice again, and he itched to do something besides sit and brood.

On pure impulse, he got up and tossed on his overcoat before heading down the stairs and out onto the sidewalk. He crossed the street and walked to the corner. Shoving through the heavy glass door, he entered the pharmacy and went to the soda counter, realizing only then that he'd hoped to find Ellie or even Kent Monroe there. Instead, he found a teenage girl with too much eye makeup and pink streaks in her hair doing homework at the counter.

She got up off her stool and moved behind the counter. "What can I get you?"

"I'll have a cappuccino root beer float."

Nodding, she went to work. He took a seat two stools down from her textbook. Moments later, she set the tall, fluted glass in front of him, a long spoon and a straw poking up through the foam. He paid the two and a half bucks that she asked for and set about demolishing his treat. By the time he was done, he felt pleasantly full— and had reached a decision of sorts.

Perhaps, he thought, he had been mistaken. Perhaps what he sensed in the Monroes was guilt for having failed to secure the house. Or perhaps he was making excuses for them because he wanted it to be that way. Regardless, he had to get to the bottom of this thing before the insurance company did. Rising, he left the pharmacy and drove straight to Chatam House.

It was pitch-black out, the gloom of the day having carried over into the evening to effectively block even the faint light of the moon and stars. Asher approached the yellow door, its brass lamps burning softly on either side.

To his surprise, Ellie answered the door. The wide, deeply cuffed neck of her oversize sweater had slipped off one smoothly rounded shoulder. She tilted her head, curls bouncing.

"Hello, Ellie. Do you have a few minutes?"

Nodding, she backed out of the doorway. "Come in. Your aunts are in their suite watching TV, I think. Grandpa and I are enjoying the fire in the front parlor."

He followed her across the foyer. Kent sat in the armchair across from the fire, staring at the dancing flames. He looked up only as Asher folded himself down into the seat next to Ellie on the settee. The older gentleman nodded.

"Asher. Didn't expect to see you again so soon."

Sighing, Asher leaned forward, his elbows braced against his knees, and clasped his hands together. "I want you to know, I've prayed about this at length and—"

"You think we set the fire," Ellie said.

Asher dropped his head. "I didn't say that. But I'm concerned about what I've heard. And about what I haven't heard from the two of you."

Ellie and her grandfather traded looks. Kent cleared his throat before saying, "I don't understand."

"Don't you? Every instinct I possess is screaming that you haven't told me everything."

"I—I can't imagine what else there is to say," Kent sputtered.

Odelia barreled into the room at that moment, wearing a blue-green-and-gold paisley caftan. "Did I hear the door? Ah. Asher. Hello, dear."

"Aunt Odelia."

She looked from one grim face to another before asking shakily, "Is everything all right?"

Kent twisted sideways in his chair. "Asher is concerned," he pronounced gravely.

"Oh. Oh, my." Eyes widening, she stepped forward. "Not about…" She glanced at Kent before bearing down on Asher. "You wouldn't…you certainly don't have to…"

"It's about the fire," Asher said in an effort to put her mind at ease.

A muscle twitched below her left eye. Gulping, she nodded. "Well, I'm sure it's none of my business, then. I'll leave you to talk. Excuse me please." Her hands fluttered at her sides. "Always blundering in where I'm not wanted," she muttered, turning away.

Kent sent Asher an accusatory glare, heaved himself up to his feet and went after her.

Asher sighed and lifted a hand to his forehead. So much for getting to the bottom of things. He couldn't press the matter now if he wanted to—and he did not, not after seeing the worry on Odelia's face and the affront on Ellie's. Neither of them would ever forgive him if he forced Kent to confess to arson, not that he'd intended to do any such thing. He couldn't reconcile the notion with what he knew of Kent Monroe. Still, something was not right, and Asher couldn't help feeling trapped between that proverbial rock and hard place, especially given his aunt's feelings for Monroe—and his feelings for Ellie.

Sitting back, he stretched an arm along the cushioned back of the settee and conceded at least part of the battle. "You're right about those two."

She relaxed, brightening visibly. "You think so? What changed your mind?"

He wouldn't break a confidence, but he didn't have to. "Did you see the way they looked at each other just now?"

She favored him with a soft smile. "I did, but I didn't think you would."

"Now, don't get your hopes up," he warned, even though he was absurdly glad to have given her even that little bit of joy. "Odelia has made it clear that she has no intention of leaving her sisters, now or ever."

"She's talked to you about him then?"

Asher nodded. "I can't betray a confidence, of course, but we have spoken about it."

"Have you counseled her not to get romantically involved?"

He looked her straight in the eye. "No, actually, I haven't."

Ellie's violet gaze studied his face for a long moment. "What are you going to do?"

"What I've been doing," he said. "Pray."

She smiled again. "Can't argue with that. I've been doing a good bit of it myself." She scrunched up her nose. "You don't suppose we're praying at cross-purposes, do you?"

"I hope not," he said sincerely. Then, strictly on impulse, he offered her his hand. "We could make sure by praying together."

Her visage softened. Eyes glowing, she slid close and put her hand in his. This, Asher knew, was right. He might not know what else to do, but this, at least, was exactly the right thing at this moment. Bowing his head and closing his eyes, he began to speak softly.

"Father God, You work all things to our good, even if sometimes it doesn't seem that way. We may not understand what is going on or why, but deep down we know that You always have our best interests at heart. Keep us mindful of that, Lord, and whatever happens, whatever comes, help us trust You to protect those we love." Ellie squeezed his hand, and he whispered, "Amen."

He looked up to find Hypatia and Magnolia standing before him, twin smiles upon their dear old faces. Magnolia wore a rumpled housecoat over a voluminous nightgown and soft corduroy slippers, her thick iron-gray braid curving across one shoulder. Hypatia was her usual tailored self in black silk pajamas, matching wrapper and foam-lined house shoes. It had been years since he'd seen her silver hair down. Caught at her nape with a band, it hung down her back between her shoulder blades.

"Do you mind if we join you?" Hypatia asked.

"Of course not," Ellie said, loosening her hand from his and sitting back.

"Please," Asher put in, standing.

"We thought we'd enjoy a cup of tea in front of the fire," Hypatia said, stepping around the wing chair opposite them to sit down. "Doesn't seem wise to build a fire in our suite at this hour when this one's already toasty warm. Won't you join us in some refreshments?"

"I'm sure there are sandwiches," Magnolia said, moving toward the door.

"And cookies," Hypatia called, hunching her shoulders in an expression of girlish delight, her amber eyes sparkling.

Asher smiled and lifted his arm to rest loosely about Ellie's shoulders. It wasn't wise, especially with the aunties already speculating about a possible romance between the two of them. Yet, he could not stop himself.

He still had to get to the bottom of the fire at

the Monroes' house, but worries and questions could wait for another day. With no small sense of contentment, he noted that Ellie relaxed beside him, her shoulder tucked into his side.

At that moment, all seemed exactly as it should, and he was in no mood to turn away that gift.

For the first time in a very long while, Asher pushed aside his concerns and simply let himself be at ease.

Chapter Twelve

Kent caught up to her in the sunroom. His Odelia was surprisingly spry, he noted, breathing heavily. No, not *his* Odelia. Not any longer, not for a very long time. And never again.

"Wait," he called. "Please."

Aiming for the door to the outside, she halted in midstep and, after a moment, turned cautiously, her beautiful eyes wide. Kent felt a kick in his chest. She was still the dearest and most beautiful woman he'd ever known—and he was obviously hurting her. He drew a deep breath, pulling in his stomach as he did so.

"I cannot bear this, Odelia," he said, his voice even more gravelly than usual. She flinched. "I cannot bear to see you so unhappy," he went on, moving closer so that he could lower his voice.

She frowned at that. "What makes you think I'm unhappy?"

He sent her a wry look. "My dear, how long have we known each other?"

"Oh, sixty years or so, I imagine," she muttered, blinking.

"Sixty-two," he corrected wistfully. "Sixty-two years, two months and three days."

He remembered it like it was yesterday, that evening when, a reluctant teenager, he had accompanied his parents to a Christmas dinner at Chatam House. Odelia and her sisters had been dressed in matching rose-red frocks heavily embroidered with holly green, their lustrous brown hair brushed and pulled back from their almost identical faces by pearl clips, the ends crimped into curls that brushed their slender shoulders. They were as alike as peas in a pod, yet it had been Odelia who had fascinated him, Odelia whom he had sought out, Odelia who had earned his heart by evening's end with her sparkling smiles, sweetness and fun spirit. Years had passed before he'd worked up the courage to try to be more than her friend and years after that before he'd gone down on his knee to her. He still could not believe that she'd agreed to marry him that day.

For a time afterward, his world had been golden and bright. When she had broken it off, he was not really surprised—she had always been too far above him—but he was almost mortally wounded. He had eventually pulled himself together and gone on with his life, marrying, becoming a father and grandfather. If not for the latter, he might now question his choices, frankly, but Ellie, dear Ellie, had been his solace and delight since the day of her birth. Not even she, however, could replace this lady in his heart, and as before, he could bear his own pain more easily than Odelia's.

"I will leave immediately, dear lady," he announced, "rather than continue to upset you with my presence and my unrequited love."

Her hands flew to her face. "Did you say…you cannot mean…after everything, can you really l-love me?"

It was his turn to be astonished. He stepped closer, reveling in her proximity. "My darling, I have loved you since I was thirteen years old. I will love you until the day I die. But I would rather love you from afar if that would make you happy again."

"Oh!" she squeaked, gazing up at him. Her warm amber eyes filled with tears. "I never dreamed that you might still care."

He bowed his head. "I have asked God so many times to take away these feelings, but for some reason He has chosen not to. And I cannot honestly say that I regret them, except for the pain they may cause you." He would have stepped away then if she had not reached out her dainty hand and grasped him by the shirt-sleeve.

"I, too, have prayed and prayed," she warbled, "trying to quiet my own feelings, but I cannot help caring for you."

"Odelia!" Kent whispered, covering her hand with his. "I don't understand. Are you saying that I must g-go…or…stay?"

"I'm saying that you will break my heart if you leave this house," she told him, leaning into his chest.

He clapped his arms around her, a familiar elation puffing up his chest. It was the same as that day he'd slipped his ring on her finger. How could it be? She even felt as she had that day, as if she fit perfectly against him. Only one thing was different: he could not quite imagine a future for them this time.

Realizing suddenly that it was the future that he had envisioned for them before that had spelled their end, he pulled himself straight, the top of her head tucked beneath his chin. Had he not been so set on living in the Monroe family home, would things have gone differently for them? The thought of being here at Chatam House, with her and her sisters and parents, had seemed unthinkable back then. He was an only child, after all, and it had always been understood that the family home would go to him. As a young man eager to begin a family of his own, he had been looking forward to setting up his household. Living with her family had seemed less than manly, but when she had said that she could never leave her sisters, he had thought that she was really saying that she could not be with him. Had he been wrong about that? If so, what did that mean for them now?

"We will pray through this together, my love," he decided, "and then we shall see what God may have in store for us."

She nodded and turned her face up to him, a smile trembling upon her lips. "Yes. Yes, let's do that."

Turning her toward one of the colorful chaises, he kept her close. It seemed to him that his feet barely touched the floor as they walked side by side toward an uncertain but hopeful future.

The house was quiet as Ellie walked Asher to the front door, the sisters having retired some time before.

"The weatherman says the front will lift tomorrow," she told him. They'd sat for long minutes in companionable silence before the fire, but now for some reason she felt compelled to speak.

"That's good." He shrugged into his overcoat. "Maybe everyone can get in a practice tomorrow."

"If we can't practice, do we still play on Saturday?"

"Depends on the fields. I'll take a look tomorrow and let everyone know by lunchtime."

She nodded. "Will I see you at the soccer field?"

He looked at the floor, thumbing the cleft in his strong chin. "I don't know." He grimaced. "Maybe."

Obviously, he was greatly conflicted about seeing her again. Still, he had come over tonight, and he hadn't, after all, pressed her about the fire. Instead, he'd prayed with her and sat with her. That was something, she supposed. It wasn't his fault that she wanted more. She backed up a step.

"Sleep well."

"For a change, you mean?" he quipped lightly. She tilted her head at that. He made a dismissive face. "Soccer season is always a busy time for me, so many details and tons of paperwork. I have a case coming up for trial soon, too."

"And now us," she said apologetically.

"And now *you*," he said, tapping the tip of her nose with his forefinger. "You worry me, Ellen Monroe. You worry me."

She didn't know what to say to that. He slipped

away before she could decide, leaving her with the bittersweet feeling that he did care for her. But would he ever care in the way she cared for him? She was beginning to believe that he could—if he would allow himself to do so.

"Nervous?"

Ellie whirled away from the soccer field where her team was loping back and forth to warm up before facing their first opponents. Many of them had worn their tutus and winged caps, to the disdain of the other team, but Asher noted that her kids were laughing and grinning while the other coach and team mother were trying to stop the rude jeers of their own players. Ellie shook her head in answer to his question.

"You came," she said, sounding so pleased that he smiled.

He'd tried not to. He really had. And he'd managed to stay away from practice, at least, but he just couldn't miss this, her first game on this bright first Saturday of March.

"No reason to be nervous," he told her.

"I know. Win or lose, what matters most to me personally is that my kids have fun."

He smiled ruefully. "They might enjoy winning."

"Better that they enjoy playing soccer," she countered.

The referee, a tall, thin, teenage boy, blew

his whistle and tapped his wristwatch before holding up five fingers. Ellie called her team in and stripped them down to their regulation uniforms, handing off the tutus and caps to a bemused Asher while the team mother passed around small bottles of water. Dropping down into a crouch, Ellie engaged every eye.

"Game faces," she instructed, demonstrating her own. She held the fierce, wooden expression for several heartbeats before breaking into a wide grin. The children followed suit, sitting solemnly then breaking into laughter. "Okay, listen to me. Just play your positions as you've learned them and don't worry about the outcome. I want you forwards taking shots on goal and not just passing to each other, and you defenders need to keep track of the ball all the time. Remember, you're in the play even if the ball isn't close to you, so be ready. Now, let's have some fun." Rising to her feet, she called out positions and names. Players popped up one by one and hit the field, high-fiving each other enthusiastically as they took their places.

"You know the other team has been playing together for a couple years now, don't you?" Asher asked softly. Despite her bravado, he desperately did not want to see her disappointed.

"I do. I also know that they don't have the skills our players do," she told him confidently.

He said nothing to that. The game would tell if she was right about that or not.

Ellie's team won the coin toss. The ref blew the whistle, and her team made a running kick-off. What followed was twenty-five minutes of chaos that somehow resolved itself into a competition.

The second half proved more settled than the first. With the score one to one, Ellie's team seemed to sense that they could win. It looked as if the contest would end in a tie, but at the last moment, a girl on Ellie's team booted a ball right into the corner of the goal. The stunned goalie of the other team stood there with his hands on his hips, glaring in disbelief while Ellie's Yellow Jackets erupted in cheers. An instant later, the ref blew his whistle. Ellie looked to Asher in astonishment.

"Did we win? Did we win?" one of the bench sitters demanded.

Asher's lips curved into a lopsided grin. "You did," he confirmed.

"We actually did!" Ellie threw her arms around Asher's neck with joy. His own arm automatically banded her waist. For a single heartbeat, they stood in an embrace, and then she straightened.

"Well done, coach," he muttered.

At almost the same moment, Ilene announced, "Ice cream sandwiches!"

Ellie's team tugged her away, but she glanced back at him. "You're right. Winning is fun!"

He bent his head to hide his grin, which grew wider with every moment. "Ellie, Ellie," he whispered. "What am I going to do with you?"

Ellie certainly hadn't expected to see Asher here today, not after he'd failed to show at practice, but she could still feel that strong arm snug about her waist even as parents overwhelmed her with their delight.

Somehow, despite the celebratory ice cream sandwiches, Ellie managed to get everyone packed up and the area vacated so that the next team could access the field. All the while, Ellie accepted a steady stream of congratulations while keeping an eye on Asher. He hung about, just a little apart from everyone else. By the time the last kid had piled into his parents' vehicle, Asher had moved to Ellie's side, his hands in his pockets. She waved until there was no one to wave at before turning to him.

"That went well, I think," she said, trying to be modest.

He laughed. "You think? I commend you on your strategy. Fun wins."

Ellie grinned. "My kids had a blast, didn't they?"

"And would have if they'd lost," he conceded.

She grinned so widely that her cheeks hurt. But then his expression sobered, and he looked down.

"Ellie, I think we should talk. Do you have a few minutes now?" Torn between hope and dread, she nodded. "Come sit in my car then," he suggested.

She followed him across the parking lot and allowed him to hand her up into the passenger-side seat before he moved around to slide beneath the steering wheel.

"Ellie," he began, reaching for her hand. For a moment he said nothing more, just smoothed the pad of his thumb across her knuckles. Her heart beat so loudly that she could barely hear him when he said, "This can't go any further."

Her heart clunked inside her chest. Had he guessed her feelings, somehow divined her dreams?

"You have to tell me what you've been holding back about the fire," he said. "I *have* to know."

Relief swamped her, followed swiftly by... guilt. She squeezed her eyes closed, praying for guidance. On one hand, she felt the need to protect her friend. On the other, she *had* omitted information. Then again, Dallas was his sister. Surely, she could trust him to help her protect her friend from any foolish behavior.

Taking a deep breath, she looked up and softly confessed, "I told Dallas we would be gone that night."

Asher's expression did not change. "Okay."

"She knew we would be at the storage unit."

He just stared at her. "And your point is?"

Ellie gulped and lost her nerve. "I—I just remembered, that's all. Thought you'd want to know."

He dropped her hand, clapping his to the nape of his neck. "Ellie, I need significant facts. You must know that you can trust me with the complete truth. I'm not just your attorney, I am also your friend. Whatever happened, whatever you or your grandfather might have done, I'll help you."

She tilted her head, telling herself that his failure to grasp the significance of what she'd told him didn't mean what she feared it did, but she would not directly accuse her friend. She'd told him what she'd kept back, and that was as far as she was prepared to go.

"You wanted to know what I hadn't told you. Now you do."

"That can't be all there is to it. Someone *arranged* that fire."

She waited for him to make the connection, but it gradually became obvious that he'd already come to a conclusion and it didn't have anything to do with what she'd told him. "You suspect Grandpa and me of setting our house on fire."

"I'm just trying to get to the truth."

"I've given you the truth."

"Ellie, you have to face facts. If you didn't set that fire—"

"I didn't!"

"Then someone else must have."

"Yes, someone else!"

"I know it's difficult, but you are a Christian woman," he began warmly. "You know that once the truth, the full truth, is out, you'll not only feel much better, but you'll be able to tap into the comfort that God is standing ready to give."

"I have told you the 'full truth'!" she snapped. "And don't you dare question my Christian ethics!"

He bowed his head and visibly, deliberately relaxed. When he looked up again, he was wearing a patently phony smile. Clapping a hand upon her shoulder, he said cajolingly, "You're too young to fully understand the situation. There are remedies, *legal* remedies, that you can't be aware of. Trust me to—"

"Trust you?" she snapped, blazingly angry now. "You discount me, disparage me, belittle me and my grandfather...you don't even listen to me! But I should *trust* you?" She yanked open the door, pivoted on her seat and slid down to the ground, whirling back to face him.

He sat stony-faced, his jaw grating. "You're behaving foolishly."

"Am I? Like a child, do you think? Well, I may be little more than a child in your book, and I may not understand as much as I think I do, but I know this—I can't trust a man who doesn't trust me."

"I'm trying to trust you," he said quietly.

"Are you? I think you're trying *not* to trust me, because that might mean that you actually care about me. Personally. But that's the one thing you won't do, isn't it? You won't care. I've got that now. And you've got the truth, whether you believe it or not, so I don't think there's any more to be said."

She slammed the door closed, turned and strode to her truck without so much as a backward glance. She dared not look back. She couldn't let him see the tears streaming down her cheeks. She couldn't let him or anyone see what it cost her to walk away from the one man she had dared to dream she might actually love.

Staring at the tall, arched, mission-style doors of the inner sanctum of the Downtown Bible Church, where Chatams had been members since its founding, Asher again considered his options and deemed them just as limited as they'd been in the middle of the previous night. He hadn't been able to sleep thinking about how horribly he'd blown it with Ellie yesterday. He couldn't forget how hurt she'd seemed, and the longer he'd thought about it, the more he'd feared that she would never speak to him again.

The idea had seemed wise at the time. He'd thought that after meeting her at the soccer field, where they obviously had something in common, he could take on the manner of a fond uncle and inspire her to tell him what he needed to know. He'd thought, too, that maintaining an avuncular attitude would help him keep his feelings in perspective.

Wrong on both counts. All he'd done was ruin her first win, insult her and drive her away—and he hadn't exactly felt like her wiser, older relative in the process. Why couldn't he have just let her enjoy her first coaching success? Because, he admitted to himself, that hug on the sideline had knocked him for a loop. Everything about Ellie seemed to knock him for a loop. The worst part of all, though, was the deep, roiling panic that he felt at the thought of never speaking to her again.

That panic astonished, humbled and troubled him. Yes, it had to do with the case. Ellie's cooperation was vital to keeping her and her grandfather out of trouble. But it was more than that. It was more than her being a family friend, too, more than her being *his* friend, so much more that he'd eat crow to mend the rift, which explained why he was here now. If he had to grovel, he might as well do it on hallowed ground.

Squaring his shoulders, Asher stepped forward and pulled open the door far enough to slip inside. The minister of education was announcing the start of a new Bible study. Asher stood at the back, oddly aware of the soaring arches, gleaming brass fixtures, stuccoed walls and stained glass windows that surrounded him.

He had known the crowd would be large at the main service, but he hadn't expected to see the backs of quite so many heads. An usher approached him then, silently offering to help him find a seat. Smiling, Asher shook his head and returned to his survey. Finally, he spied her, more than halfway down. She sat three people in from the end of the pew, her grandfather on her left, Asher's uncle Hub on her right, with his cousin Kaylie and her husband Stephan on the outside.

As Asher made his way down the side of the church, he noted that Kent sat next to Odelia, who wore an enormous pink, feathered hat. A pair of bluebirds almost large enough to be real swung from her earlobes as if attempting to land on her yellow-clad shoulders. He smiled, despite his disquiet. It looked as if his dear old auntie was back to her eccentric self. Glancing at Kent, who leaned in to whisper something in her ear, Asher felt a spurt of alarm on her behalf. What would happen to his sweet aunt if it turned out that her old beau was responsible for the fire at his house? Telling himself that he had enough worries of his own at the moment, Asher stopped at the end of the pew, sent Stephan Gallow an apologetic glance and stepped over the big man's enormous feet.

A professional hockey player, Stephan sent a glower his way, then smiled as if to say that it was nothing more than habit before shifting aside. Asher nodded at Kaylie then jerked his head sideways to suggest that she move down. She sent a bemused glance toward the other end of the crowded pew and snuggled up next to her husband. It occurred to Asher as he struggled past his surprised uncle that Kaylie couldn't be much older than Ellie. Yet there she sat, happily married. He wondered just how old Stephan was. Not as old as him, surely, he thought, placing a hand on his uncle's arm to let him know that he wanted to squeeze in next to Ellie, who only then looked his way.

A frown turned down the corners of her mouth, and she moved as far from him as possible, all but turning her back on him. He wedged himself into the small space, stretching his arm out along the back of the pew in order to give himself more room, and leaned in close to whisper pleadingly, "Ellie."

She twisted slightly, jabbing her elbow into his ribs. "I don't want to talk to you," she whispered, "now that I know you're not on our side."

"I am," he softly insisted.

Suddenly she launched herself to her feet. Music erupted, and he realized that somehow, he had missed the call to worship as well as the announcement of the first song. Rising belatedly, he allowed himself to really gaze at Ellie. He almost wished he hadn't indulged the impulse.

She looked achingly beautiful in a strawberry-red sheath. She'd caught her hair up on top of her head somehow, leaving curly little tendrils to fall about her face and nape. Tiny ruby studs adorned her delicate earlobes.

"I'm sorry," he whispered in her ear.

She ignored him.

"I only want to help you," he said.

Nothing.

"Please don't be mad at me."

She sent him a speaking glance, her eyes so sad that it was all he could do not to take her in his arms right then. Instead, he lifted a hand to help her support the hymnal that she held and listened as she began to sing. She had a credible alto voice. After a moment, he joined his own limited baritone to hers, singing as much in supplication as praise.

Chapter Thirteen

Ellie did her dead-level best not to so much as glance in Asher's direction again throughout the remainder of the service, but she sensed that he was as aware of her as she was of him. She resented that he had cornered her, literally, in church. Maybe he really did feel bad about offending her, but that didn't change the fact that he suspected her of arson. He had to know that if he'd approached her elsewhere, she'd have told him to get lost, but she couldn't do that in the midst of a worship service. She didn't have to acknowledge him, though, and spent most of the time talking silently to God.

Lord, I don't want to be angry, but he thinks I started that fire! Do I have to spell it out for him? And what about Grandpa? How could he suspect my grandpa of something like that? Especially now, especially after Asher kissed me.

Oh, it was best not to go there. That kiss had meant nothing, less than nothing. Why, it had been downright insulting. He had apologized for it, for pity's sake. How much more proof did she need that… Wait a minute. Had that kiss been about softening her up so she'd confess? Was that why he'd sat by the fireside with her, casting her those poignant looks and holding her hand while he'd prayed?

Suddenly incensed, she shifted to sit on one hip in order to present her back to him as much as possible.

"Ellie," he whispered pleadingly.

She stared straight ahead, but she didn't hear one word that the pastor said. Later, when the congregation rose for the closing hymn, she was among the last to get to her feet. Immediately, she shifted to her left, intent on putting as much distance between them as possible, only to feel his arm slip around her waist and pull her close to his side. Stiffening, she pretended not to notice.

As they filed out into the central aisle behind his aunties and her grandfather a few minutes later, she did her best to move away from him, but Asher made certain to stay close, his hand curled around the curve of her waist. She attempted to walk ahead of him, but his hand went with her and the rest of him caught up.

Eventually they made it to the cavernous foyer,

and she slipped free. The Chatam sisters were there ahead of them, of course, along with her grandfather and Asher's uncle and cousin and her husband. It felt very much as if they were waiting for her and Asher. She saw the curiosity and speculation in their eyes, but before she could escape, Odelia stepped forward.

"Asher, dear, what a delight to see you here this morning. You'll take lunch with us at Chatam House, of course. Won't you?" Surprised because the aunties usually "ate simple" on Sundays so the household staff could have the day off, Ellie blinked. Then Odelia turned a worshipful gaze on Ellie's grandfather and crooned, "Kent grilled for us yesterday. Isn't that lovely?"

Asher's eyebrows rose. He cleared his throat and said, "That sounds great."

"Chicken and pineapple kebabs," Kent announced proudly. "Warming in the kitchen even as we speak."

Ellie targeted her gaze on her shoes to keep from glaring at him. She hadn't told her grandfather about Asher's suspicions because she hadn't wanted to upset him, so naturally he thought everything was fine. Well, that didn't mean she had to be welcoming of Asher. Let the others do that. She edged toward the exit, but Asher's hand shot out and fastened about her wrist. She either had to fight him for it or stand still. Fuming, she stood still.

"I'd love to join you for lunch," Asher said formally.

Nodding with approval, the aunties extended the luncheon invitation to Hub, Kaylie and Stephan. "Oh, no, thank you," Hub refused for them all. "Kaylie has a pot roast in the slow cooker."

The sisters took their leave of their brother and his daughter and son-in-law with hugs and pats.

"We'll see you at the house then, Asher," Magnolia called as they trundled away. Her grandfather went with them. He'd driven the town car that morning so Chester, the Chatams' houseman and driver, who had a mild cold, could stay in. Ellie could have gone along, but she'd preferred to make the short trip alone. She hadn't been in the mood for company since she'd spoken with Asher the day before. Silently, she jerked on her arm, but he held fast.

"Ride with me."

She shook free. "I drove my truck."

"Your grandfather could—"

"He's driving the town car," she said dismissively, very aware of Asher's surprise. She didn't wait around for his response. Instead, she walked away without another word, leaving Asher to figure things out for himself.

* * *

"Well, that's a first," Asher muttered, watching Ellie walk away.

"It's been a morning of firsts," his cousin Kaylie said.

Asher turned to find her, her husband and his uncle staring at him as if he'd grown a second head. Kaylie's eyes twinkled merrily as she glanced at Ellie's retreating figure and then at him. "What?"

Hub cleared his throat. "First, Kent is driving the town car."

"Chester has a cold," Kaylie supplied helpfully.

"Then we learn that the Monroes have been staying at Chatam House for weeks!" Hub declared.

"I'm afraid we've neglected the aunts a bit," Kaylie said apologetically. "It's just been so busy, finally moving into the new house, traveling to hockey games…"

"It's the middle of the season," Stephan explained.

"And now this," Kaylie said, waving a dainty hand to indicate Asher's presence. "Do I detect a ro—"

"Don't say it," Asher growled, striding past her.

"What?" he heard Hub ask.

"The *R* word," Stephan muttered.

"What *R* word?"

"Romance," Kaylie answered succinctly, her laughter tinkling like chimes in the soaring space as Asher strode across the foyer. "It's what happens at Chatam House."

Wincing, Asher hurried out into the cool, cloudy day to his vehicle. Kaylie was right. And wrong. There was a romance afoot. It just wasn't his. He imagined the family's shock if Odelia and Kent did marry.

He felt a pang at the idea, and not because Odelia was his aunt or they were older. He thought of how Kaylie had fallen in love with Stephan while he was recovering from an accident at Chatam House and of how happy they seemed together. For the first time in his life, he knew the bereft, sinking bite of envy.

That didn't mean that he and Ellie were destined to follow suit. He cared about Ellie. She was a bright, beautiful, creative, unique woman, but even if he had been convinced that he should try marriage again—and he wasn't—she was a client and too young for him. Those were the facts, plain and simple. His personal ethic demanded that he keep those facts in mind. Even if he had kissed her.

So what, he asked himself, was doing? What compelled him to pursue Ellie like a lion running down a gazelle? He had apologized. For perfectly reasonable behavior, given the circumstances. Shouldn't that be the end of it? Why couldn't he leave it at that?

He asked himself those questions throughout the midday meal—an odd affair, to say the least. Ellie could not have been more uncomfortable. But Hypatia and Magnolia seemed as oblivious to that fact as they were to the way that Odelia blossomed beneath the fawning attention that Kent poured over her. Asher watched in astonishment as his old auntie twinkled, giggled, fluttered her eyelashes, laughed and teased. Perhaps her behavior wasn't so different from normal— she was known for her ebullience, after all—but it had been weeks since she'd been her old self.

Kent had attention only for Odelia and so did not seem to notice that Ellie ate in withdrawn silence. More accurately, she pushed her food around on her plate without ever glancing up or speaking a word, when she should have been smugly happy at the byplay going on between her grandfather and Odelia.

When, at length, Odelia pushed back her chair and announced that she was going to help Kent look for his cat, her sisters seemed almost relieved, perhaps even eager, to get her and everyone else out of the way.

"I'll help you clean up," Ellie murmured, speaking for the first time.

"Oh, no," Magnolia objected, rising to her feet. Asher dropped his fork and shot up in an attempt to maintain the aunties' exacting standard of polite behavior.

"We'll just carry everything into the kitchen, put away the leftovers and stack the dishes in the washer," Hypatia said. "It won't take long."

"In that case," Ellie said, getting up, "I'd like a private word with Asher."

Surprised but pleased by that turn of events, Asher gladly followed her from the large, dark dining room into the library.

"Thank you," he began before she even turned from closing the door. "I want to apologize again for—"

"Your services are no longer needed," she interrupted bluntly.

Stunned into silence, he could only stand there gawking while she folded her arms, strode farther into the room and parked herself on the edge of the mahogany library table.

"I haven't spoken to my grandfather yet," she went on, "but I'll have to tell him what you said yesterday."

Asher clapped a hand to the back of his neck, trying to think. "A-about that, you misunderstood what I was trying to say. Whatever you might think, I am on your side, and I do care ab—"

"Goodbye, Asher." She abruptly launched herself toward the door.

Before he knew what he was doing, he'd grabbed her by the arm and spun her around. "You can't fire me!"

"I just did."

"For yourself, maybe, but not for your grandfather!"

"Fine. I'll let Grandpa fire you himself, but you no longer represent me!"

"Is that right?"

"That's right."

"Good enough!" he exclaimed, angered beyond reason. What did she want, for pity's sake? He'd apologized. Repeatedly. For perfectly logical behavior. He'd turned himself inside out trying to protect her. And she fired him? Well, that changed everything. "If you're no longer my client, then I can do this." He yanked her to him and pressed a kiss onto her lips.

A heartbeat later, they sprang apart, both gasping, each trying to gauge the reaction of the other. After a moment, she tugged her jacket into place and lifted her chin before leisurely turning to stroll toward the door once more. But then she paused to look back at him.

"You're still fired, by the way."

With that, she walked out the door.

Being fired, he thought, watching the door close behind her, was the least of his problems!

If she'd had any idea how he'd react, Ellie mused, she'd have fired Ash long ago. She had not dared hope that he felt as drawn to her as she did to him, and then yesterday after the game, when he'd seemed intent on squeezing a confession out of her, she'd been angry and hurt. Now she wondered if perhaps he *needed* to suspect her of culpability in the fire in order to protect himself from his own feelings. She was still miffed about that, but somehow, after this latest kiss, it seemed much easier to forgive him. Besides, wasn't she as guilty of assigning guilt to Dallas for that fire as Asher was of suspecting her and her grandfather?

Up in her room, curled around a pillow on her bed, Ellie relived that kiss repeatedly. In the process, she talked the situation over with God. Being with Asher seemed so right to her, so entirely what she was supposed to do. On the other hand, she could very well be building castles in the air. It was so easy to mistake one's own desires for God's will, and she earnestly wanted what God wanted for her. What good was getting her own way if it was going to make her unhappy in the end?

She'd learned that lesson from her grandmother, God rest her. Deirdre Billups Monroe had set her cap for her husband long before he'd ever looked her way and only after he'd given up hope of marrying his first love, Odelia. According to Deirdre herself, Kent had been blatant about his feelings, but Deirdre had been determined to have him. Eventually she had convinced him that they were each other's only chance at making a family, or so Kent had told her. Sadly, though, over time the knowledge that he'd loved another had eaten up Deirdre's love for him. Deirdre had gotten her way, but she'd been unhappy with the results. Ellie was determined not to be so foolish.

It still surprised Ellie that her father had married a woman so like his own mother. It seemed that he had learned how to love from his own dad and how to *be* loved from his mother. Ellie hoped that she had learned better. Her dad and grandpa had shown her what sort of man she wanted to love her, and her mother and grandmother had shown her what sort of wife and mother she did *not* want to be.

But what if she could not be better than them and God knew it? What if this was all just history repeating itself? What if she was hung up on a man who couldn't truly care for her because he couldn't get past the failure of his first attempt at love?

These things went around and around in her thoughts until a remembered bit of favorite Scripture, Psalm 20:4, brought clarity.

May He give you the desire of your heart and make all your plans succeed.

That was what she had prayed for her grandfather for years now, for if the fulfillment of one's heart's desire came from God, rather than simply from one's self, then it was the right, best thing.

Finding a measure of peace at last, Ellie sat up. She had no idea what would happen next, but it was all in God's hands, just as it should be. If that kiss meant anything at all, then surely Asher would act upon it. If not, well, she wouldn't be any worse off than before, would she? At least she had finally unburdened herself about Dallas. If Asher hadn't made the connection, well, then perhaps, please God, there weren't any connections to be made.

She scrambled off the bed and went to brush her hair, knowing that the Chatam sisters would expect her to show up in the common areas of the house looking her best. Just as she laid the brush atop the dresser, she heard a bustle in the sitting room.

"Careful. Careful!" came Odelia's voice.

Curious and surprised, Ellie went to the door of her room. Her grandfather was gingerly placing a cardboard box on the coffee table standing in front of the cream-white sofa. Glancing up, he motioned her closer.

"We found him, Ellie. We found old Curly!"

"You found the cat?" She rushed forward.

"Odelia found him," Kent said, carefully beginning to fold back the flaps on the box. "He was upstairs in my room."

"Upstairs!"

"In my room," Kent confirmed, folding back the last flap.

"All this time?"

Ellie peered into the box. A rag-and-bones Curly lay atop a soiled towel, his dark eyes rolling. Not only had he lost weight, patches of charred black and raw red marred his mottled yellow fur.

"Don't touch him," Kent warned. "He's been injured, poor old thing."

Ellie studied the cat's hide. "Grandpa, that cat's been burned!"

"Yes, that's what I figure, too."

"Don't you see what this could mean?"

"Yes, of course. It's very serious. Though if he's lived this long, I expect he'll make it."

Ellie clapped a hand down onto her grandfather's shoulder. "It means that the cat was in the house when the fire started. Grandpa, it means that Curly could have started the fire!"

Kent reared back. "But…how?"

"He must've come through the open window," Ellie theorized. "He could've knocked over the bucket while using it to jump up onto the sofa table."

"And then knocked over the lamp," Kent mused.

"It wouldn't be the first time he'd done that," Ellie pointed out excitedly. "But it would be the first time for the paint thinner."

Kent dropped down onto the sofa. "Good grief, that's the answer."

"We must tell Asher," Odelia pointed out, patting Kent's shoulder.

"Yes, yes, you're right." He looked to Ellie. "You'll take care of it, won't you, dear?"

Ellie rocked back on her heels. "Oh, um, you should talk to Asher about this. He's *your* attorney, and this is official business, so to speak."

"Ah. Well, if you think that best."

He traded a look with Odelia, who said brightly, "I'll just call my nephew Reeves and find out which veterinarian he uses for his daughter's cat." After patting Kent's shoulder again, she hurried away, leaving Ellie to smile serenely at her grandfather.

"I'm sure Curly will recover. It's been a while already, as you said, and he's still with us, after all."

"So he is," Kent acknowledged, nodding. He

leaned over the box and crooned, "I think this warrants a dish of cream, old man. Don't you?"

"Well, I'll just let Dallas know the news," Ellie said, moving toward her bedroom.

Closing the box, her grandfather rose. He smiled at Ellie, a look of compassion in his eyes. "You do that, sweet girl, and I'll take care of her brother."

It appeared that he understood only too well that she was avoiding Asher. He couldn't know why, of course, but he had to realize that a rift had opened between them. What no one but God Almighty could know was whether that kiss had served to bridge that fracture in any way.

"Thank you, Grandpa," Ellie answered softly. *May He give you the desire of your heart and make all your plans succeed,* she thought. *Even if He doesn't do the same for me.*

Chapter Fourteen

Bowing his head over his desk, Asher pressed the fingertips of both hands to his aching temples. He had not slept well. Again. Every time he'd closed his eyes, that kiss had played through his mind. To make matters worse, he'd repeatedly confessed his foolishness in instigating the event but had never quite felt absolved. It felt, in fact, as if God was laughing at him. Well, chuckling, anyway, as if to say that he was old enough to know better than to get himself into this mess. In desperation, Asher had resorted to enumerating all the reasons why a romance with Ellie Monroe was a bad idea. He felt the need to run down the list again now.

One, he'd already tried and failed at being half of a couple. Two, she was not the sort of woman he'd ever envisioned pairing up with— not that he'd envisioned pairing up with anyone in a very long time. Three, quirky was not a trait he'd ever valued. Four, he hardly even knew the girl, really! Even if he somehow felt that he did. Five, she interrupted everyone. Six, she was too young. Seven, she could be an arsonist. Okay, he didn't really believe that, but no lawyer worth his salt would entirely discount the possibility. Eight, she was almost painfully beautiful, and why he hadn't realized that before he couldn't understand.

No, wait. Scratch that last.

Frowning, Asher bludgeoned his mind for the remainder of the list. At times he'd gotten as far as twelve, but somehow during the night he'd lost a few of those reasons. What really troubled him, though, was that he could feel his will to keep Ellie at arm's length going the same way.

When Barb buzzed him to say that Kent Monroe had "dropped by for a word," Asher figured that he need not worry about keeping Ellie at a distance any longer. He fully expected that Kent would walk in, fire him and walk out again. He told himself that he was relieved, but the way his gut roiled put the lie to that. The last thing he expected was the beaming bonhomie with which the older man greeted him.

"Asher, my boy, great news! Great news!"

Surprised, Asher didn't even make it all the way to his feet. Kent bustled across the room and dropped down into the armchair in front of the desk, grinning broadly.

"It was the cat," he said the instant that Asher's behind touched the chair seat again.

"Pardon?"

"We found him, my old tom, Curly, holed up licking his wounds. Burns," he clarified significantly, crossing his thick legs. "Vet says he'll mend, though he probably won't have hair in places." Kent waved that away, explaining all that he'd discovered.

Listening, Asher's understanding grew. He smacked himself in the forehead with the heel of his hand. "That's it. That's the answer."

Kent made a wiping motion across his own forehead. "Whew! That's a relief, I don't mind telling you." He shifted in his chair, adding, "Fact is, I can't rightly remember turning on the lamp that night. Then again, I forgot to lock the front door, didn't I? Odelia says the shock of the fire has confounded my brain."

Asher thought it best not to comment on that statement. Instead, he glanced at the clock and reached for his electronic address book. "I'll call the insurance company today."

"Yes, yes. The sooner the better. Again, I can't tell you how relieved I am. To tell you the truth, I haven't been entirely forthcoming with you."

Asher set aside the handheld gadget, his senses pricking. "No. Really?"

If Kent suspected sarcasm, he didn't signal as much. Grimacing, he said, "I took out a private mortgage."

Asher sat back in his chair. "Ah." No wonder the insurance adjustor had hinted at financial impropriety.

"Just a small one," Kent went on. "Less than fifteen thousand. I didn't have the cash to finish the renovations, you see, but I didn't want Ellie to know. It's all for her, for her inheritance, but she never thinks of herself and wouldn't have wanted me to go into debt." He tilted his head, saying in his gravelly voice, "I hope you won't tell her."

Asher shook his head. "Let's just leave Ellie out of this, shall we? She fired me, anyway."

Kent's bushy eyebrows leapt upward. "What?"

"We, um, had a difference of opinion," Asher confessed, feeling the burn of guilt. "Actually, I offended her, and she fired me. I no longer represent her."

"I'm sure it's just a misunderstanding," Kent murmured, obviously troubled.

"I'll understand if you'd prefer to let someone else handle things from here on out," Asher offered carefully. To his relief, Kent shook his head.

"No, no, no. I'm sure you'll work out your

differences between you. Besides, we could be family soon, you and I."

Asher reared back in shock. Kent couldn't really expect him to marry Ellie. Could he? They hadn't even been out on a date! "What makes you say that?"

Kent Monroe squared his shoulders and set both feet flat on the floor. "I should tell you bluntly that I intend, very soon, to…again…ask your dear aunt to marry me."

Asher worked hard at keeping his expression placid. Of course. He should have expected that. "I see. Well, since we're being blunt, I feel I should warn you that Aunt Odelia has told me, quite recently, that she has no intention of ever leaving her sisters."

Kent waved that away with a swipe of his hand. "I'm not a man who makes the same mistake twice. If she doesn't want to leave Chatam House, then we won't. My house is going to Ellie anyway." Kent shifted in his seat and added, "I had thought to give it to the two of you."

Nothing Asher could do would keep his jaw in place. "I beg your p-pardon?"

Kent leaned forward. "I admit I've been distracted, but a blind man could see that the two of you have feelings for each other."

Asher rubbed his ear in an effort to hide his

embarrassment. That obvious, was it? What was just as obvious was that Kent Monroe approved.

"You should hear the way she speaks of you," Kent told him. "I don't think she even realizes she's doing it. 'Ash will take care everything.' 'Ash is so generous.' 'Ash says this, Ash says that.' I've never heard the like from her."

She called him "Ash" in private, did she? Only his closest friends and family called him that. It thrilled him to know that she thought of him that way. But that didn't really change anything, did it?

He met Kent Monroe's frank gaze. "You don't think I'm too old for her?"

Kent looked surprised. "I've always thought that an adult is an adult."

Clearly, in Kent's mind, his granddaughter was an adult. That made it difficult for Asher to hold on to the idea that Ellie was too young for him. And she wasn't his client anymore, either. That meant that the only thing standing between them was...

What shall we call this, Lord? he asked silently. *Caution? Fear? My own stiff-necked stupidity?* Whatever it was, maybe it was time to get it out of the way.

For Kent Monroe, he had only a smile and a wish. "May you know every happiness, sir, and my aunt along with you."

They both got to their feet and shook hands before Asher walked the older man to the door. As soon as Kent had gone, Asher turned back to his desk and picked up the phone. He had plans to make.

Three days, Ellie thought. Three days since that kiss. She'd hoped that he would show up at the Monday practice, but he'd been conspicuously absent, and she hadn't seen any sign of him on this Wednesday afternoon, either. If he was going to come see her, he'd have done so by now. No, she had to face facts.

Two of her kids were hip-bumping when they should have been paying attention to the ball.

"Chuck, Miguel, eyes on the prize!" she called.

Asher might be attracted to her, but he was apparently able to put her out of mind easily enough, while she couldn't seem to stop thinking about him. Well, what had she expected? Hadn't she known all along that she wasn't the sort of woman to inspire devotion in a man like him? Or perhaps any man?

Keeping the kids on task seemed to require a huge effort of will, but Ellie managed to stumble through the lengthy scrimmage.

"Good job!" she praised when it was time to pack it in. "I'll see y'all on Friday," she called, as the kids ran off the field.

"Turned out to be a pretty day," Ilene commented, shoving balls into a net bag while Ellie swigged down a bottle of water Ilene had handed her.

"Um-hm."

She hadn't really noticed, but the sun was out and the sky was clear on a day so mild that the temperature didn't even register with her. Hadn't it been gray earlier? She couldn't remember. Her mood was so gray that it probably colored everything around her. Sighing, she turned to help Ilene carry the cooler to the trunk of her car. They were halfway there when she saw him.

Dressed in a brown suit and a white shirt with an open collar, Asher stood next to his SUV in the distance, ankles crossed as he leaned against the fender. Ellie stumbled, and in the instant required to right herself, he pushed away from the vehicle, starting toward her with a long, loose-limbed stride.

They reached the rear of Ilene's car and lifted the cooler into the trunk. Ellie turned away as Ilene started loading kids into the backseat.

"See you Friday."

"See you."

Walking over to her truck, Ellie pulled her keys from the pocket of her shorts and unlocked the driver's door. Then she simply stood there and waited for him.

"What's up?" she asked as he drew near, determined to show him that she had maintained an even keel despite that kiss.

He reached inside his coat and pulled out a dollar bill. "I came to return this," he told her, holding it out.

Frowning, she shook her head. "I don't understand."

"It's your retainer. Now that we've ended our professional relationship, I need to return it."

She rolled her eyes. "I think we can agree that you've earned your retainer."

"Take it, Ellie. To ease my mind."

"To ease your mind?" she said angrily. "Is that what this is about? Well, let me do that by telling you that the cat did it. The stupid cat started the fire." The slightest of smiles curved his lips, but he just waved the dollar bill. "You already knew, didn't you?" she realized.

Reaching for her hand, he turned it palm up and plopped the bill into it. She curled her fingers around it, eyeing him as he smoothly told her, "I am ethically constrained from discussing cases with anyone but my clients." He leaned forward slightly and reminded her, "You are no longer my client."

"Fine," she snapped, clasping the top of the truck door in preparation for sliding into the cab.

He covered her hand with his, halting her in

midaction. "I'd be happy to discuss the ethics of my profession with you."

Like she needed a lecture on why he regretted kissing her and wanted to keep his distance. "Sorry," she told him. "I happen to be really hungry at the moment."

"That actually works well for me," he said. "We'll have dinner."

"Dinner," Ellie echoed stupidly. She glanced down at herself. "I don't think so. I'm not exactly dressed to go out for dinner. Unless you intend to do a drive-through."

"Actually, I have something else in mind. And you're perfectly dressed for it."

Ellie blinked. So, this had to do with soccer after all. "Okay. Where are we going?"

"Why don't you just ride along with me," he suggested, taking her by the arm. "I'll bring you back to your truck later."

She glanced around at the busy parking lot. There were a few empty spaces, so she supposed she wouldn't be putting anyone out by leaving her truck here for an hour or so. Shrugging, she backed out of the truck and locked the door.

He walked her to his SUV and handed her up inside before taking his place behind the steering wheel.

"So how did practice go?"

"Pretty well," she said, not interested in providing further details. Asher got the message.

They drove in silence until Ellie realized that they had left the business district behind and were instead driving through his neighborhood.

"Where is this restaurant we're going to?"

"Who said anything about a restaurant?" Asher asked lightly, making the turn into the drive. She realized that they'd pulled up behind his house when he hit a button overhead and the garage door started to go up.

"So it's a dinner meeting at your place?"

"That's right."

He pulled the truck into the garage, killed the engine and got out. Ellie slipped out on her side before he could come around to open the door. He went to the door that led into the house. She glanced around her, noting that his garage was neater than most people's living rooms.

She followed him into a dark, narrow hallway that led past a sizable laundry and a small powder room to the kitchen. Backtracking to the laundry, she quickly stepped out of her cleats, returning to the kitchen in her stocking feet. He stood peering into the refrigerator when she got back.

"How do you feel about an omelet?" he asked. "It's that or a sandwich, and I can't vouch for how long this sliced turkey's been here."

Ellie froze in the act of sliding up onto a tall

chair placed at the kitchen bar. "What had you planned to fix?"

"I hadn't planned anything," he told her, taking out a tray of eggs.

Now, wasn't that just like a man! "Well, how many are you expecting?"

He cast her a dry look. "We're all here."

Ellie hopped down off the chair she'd just settled on. "You mean it's just the two of us?"

Asher placed the eggs on the counter, then braced his hands against it. "Listen, Ellie. Let's just scramble up some eggs and see where that takes us. Okay?"

Her heart fluttered and began slamming inside her chest. "Yeah. Okay. I can go with that."

He took down a bowl and started cracking eggs into it. "There's a game on TV if you want to go into the other room and turn on the set."

"Oh, ah, why don't you handle that and let me take care of the eggs?"

Smiling, he dropped the eggshells as if they were hot rocks. "Look around for whatever you need. I'll be right back."

His shoulder brushed hers as he passed by on his way into the living room. Ellie stayed where she was for a moment, then carefully moved around the bar to the island countertop where the eggs awaited her.

No promises, Asher had said, but maybe some answered prayer.

* * *

They ate eggs scrambled with green onions, black olives, bits of ham and sour cream that she'd found in the refrigerator. Asher got down plates that they filled and carried into the living room, where they watched a South American match, sitting side by side on his sofa.

She was having such a good time that she forgot completely about those at Chatam House until her grandfather called her cell phone. He brushed aside her apologies and didn't seem at all surprised when she told him that she was with Asher.

"At any rate, I'll be home by nine," she promised.

"I won't wait up if you're later," he said, unconcerned.

"I won't be. Tomorrow's a school day."

"Aw, but you're the teacher, not the student."

"Which means that I have to be there earlier than anyone else."

After she'd hung up, Asher asked, "Has your grandfather spoken to you about Odelia?"

"Not really. They're spending a lot of time together, though, and he seems happy."

Asher just nodded at that.

Once the game ended, they carried their plates back into the kitchen and loaded them into the dishwasher, which was half-full. Explaining that he normally only ran the appliance once a week, Asher scrubbed out the skillet that she'd used.

When that was done, he glanced at his wristwatch. "Better scoot if we're going to get you home by curfew."

She rolled her eyes. Then she saw that he was grinning. She went to the laundry room, thoroughly confused, to get into her shoes. He waited in the hallway then followed her out to the garage. This time he insisted on opening the car door for her.

What was going on here?

They drove back to the soccer field, which was dark and deserted. He got out and walked her to her truck. Opening the door, she started to slide into the cab.

"Not so fast," he said. Lifting her hand from the truck door, he stepped to the side, drawing her out from behind it. "I want to be clear about something. Tonight was not a date."

Ellie tamped down her disappointment, saying lightly, "Believe me, Asher, you've made it clear for some time now that our spending time together is not 'a date.' But I enjoyed myself anyway."

"Excellent. Enough to try the real thing?"

"The real thing," she echoed uncertainly, standing at arm's length.

"Dinner," he said. "In a restaurant this time.

Oh, and a movie." A slow smile stretched his lips. "Not on the same night, mind you. Thought I'd nail down the second date now."

Elation swept through Ellie as she allowed him to reel her in. "You're asking me out on a real date?"

"Two dates," he corrected. "I refuse to be a one-date discard, and for the record, I'd like several more dates after that."

Tears gathered in Ellie's eyes. "Seriously?"

"Seriously. Now, what do you say?"

Stepping close, she wrapped her arms around him and laid her head on his shoulder. "Dinner. Movie. Every date after that. I accept them all."

He chuckled and shifted so that her head was tucked neatly beneath his chin. "I've been alone a long time, Ellie, and I wasn't any good at being with someone before."

"Maybe it was the wrong someone."

"Maybe. And maybe I was the wrong someone. I don't know. But I want to try to be the right someone for you, Ellie."

She slipped her arms around him. "I think you can do anything you want to do."

He laughed. "From your lips to God's ears, sweetheart. From your lips to God's ears."

She closed her eyes and smiled. That was one thing he didn't have to worry about. God would continue to hear from her regularly—she had much to be thankful for.

They went to dinners. Plural. They went to movies. Again, plural. They went to soccer games and soccer meetings and soccer practices. They even went to church together.

At times, Asher felt sure he'd lost his mind, but those times were invariably when he was away from Ellie. When they were together, all seemed just as it should be. He noticed that she didn't interrupt him anymore. He also noticed that he seemed to smile more often. And eventually he noticed that his little sister seemed rather subdued.

Being with Ellie had given him a new perspective on Dallas, and he began to think that he might have sold Dallas short, so to speak. Consequently, when the opportunity arose to engage her in meaningful conversation, he took it gladly.

They met on the front porch of Chatam House at the very end of March. He was coming; she was going.

"No romance going on under this roof," she quipped drily, and would have swept right by him, but he snagged her by the arm and turned her back to face him.

"Where are you off to?"

She shrugged. "Nowhere in particular. But Ellie has a date. With you. Again. And Odelia's gone off somewhere. Mags is working out in the greenhouse, so Hypatia is catching up on some paperwork having to do with the BCBC scholarship fund or something like that. No reason to hang around here."

He tugged her toward the chairs where he'd sat with Odelia one dark night a few weeks ago. "Sit down a minute. I have something to say."

Sighing gustily, she stomped over and dropped down onto the seat of one chair. Asher folded himself down into the chair next to her and leaned forward.

"I think I owe you an apology."

Her jaw dropped, which made him laugh. She pointed a finger at him. "You are apologizing to me?" She shook her head. "Well, that's one for the books. What exactly are you apologizing for? No, wait. Doesn't matter. This is still a red-letter day. I'm going to go home and write it on my calendar with a red marker. 'Ash apologized to me today.'"

Chuckling, he patted her on the knee. "I've discounted you, sis," he said. "Put you down as an overgrown teenager. I've mocked your romantic ideals and dismissed your ambitions. I was wrong to do that. In my defense, all I can say is that you're my baby sister and maybe I've wanted to keep you that way. I haven't wanted to let you grow up. But, of course, you have, anyhow."

"Is there a camera crew hiding around here somewhere?" she joked, glancing around suspiciously. "I'm going to see this on TV next week, aren't I?"

"Only if you're filming it yourself," he said, getting to his feet. "Now get out of here. You're making me late for my date, you know."

He turned toward the door, only to turn back at the sound of his name.

"Ash."

"Yeah?"

"Thanks."

He just smiled and started to turn away again.

"She loves you, Ash."

His heart stopped, then stuttered and took off again. Sucking in a deep breath, he looked his sister in the eye. "I believe she does."

"And?"

"And," he said, reaching for the doorknob, "I'll get back to you on that."

She made a disappointed sound, dropping her shoulders and lightly stomping one foot. He just laughed at her and opened the door. There were some things that a baby sister ought not to be the first to know.

On the other hand…

Standing there in the foyer of the ancestral Chatam family home, the staid attorney discovered that he might be something of a romantic, after all.

Chapter Fifteen

Sitting on the edge of the porch at Chatam House, Ellie tucked her A-line skirt around her thighs and crossed her legs at the ankles on the step below. She'd donned the skirt over her shorts because it feminized the silky, red polo-style top that she'd bought to match the colors of Ash's select team. Adjusting the thin, red elastic band that held back her curly hair, she sighed happily.

Her team had won again that morning for the third Saturday in a row, despite a stiff early April wind that had played havoc with the ball. Asher had been on hand to see it. Now she waited for him to pick her up for an evening match between his select team and another club in Dallas.

Smiling to herself, she braced her elbows atop her knees and parked her chin in her up-turned palms, enjoying the colorful sunset as she anticipated Ash's arrival. They'd been in each other's company a good deal these past several weeks, and she was hopelessly, unabashedly in love, though she dared not say it. He was much more fun and lighthearted than anyone else knew, yet also steady, careful and responsible— maybe too much so to commit himself permanently to a zany woman like her.

Her smile faltered.

Despite all the "second dates," as Ash called them, she still worked against getting her hopes up. Even if nothing ever came of the time they'd spent together, though, she knew that she would never regret it. Ash was everything she'd ever wanted, but she couldn't quite imagine that he would feel the same way about her. It could be, likely would be, that he'd move on soon to some woman nearer his own age, someone who had more in common with him than kids' soccer. If so, then at least she could take joy in having proved to him that the possibility of love remained a reality. She could say, if only to herself, that God had used her to reawaken the heart of a good man.

The familiar white SUV turned into the drive and accelerated up the slope. When it reached the circle, it veered right. Straightening, Ellie lifted a hand to wave in welcome. As the vehicle came to an abrupt halt, she rose and nervously adjusted the line of her skirt.

Asher practically leapt out and came loping around the front bumper. Taking the steps in one long stride, he snagged her hand and towed her toward the front door.

"What's going on?"

"I have news," he said, amber eyes twinkling, "good news."

"About what?" she asked, laughing as he opened the door and pulled her through it into the foyer.

He towed her into the front parlor, where the Chatam sisters lingered over their ubiquitous cups of tea. All three rose to their feet, Hypatia turning, as the newcomers burst into the room.

"Asher, dear." She switched her gaze back and forth between him and Ellie, pressing her hands together. "I sense an announcement."

"The insurance company has settled." He looked down at Ellie, adding, "They've offered a generous amount, very generous."

Obviously disappointed, the sisters traded looks. Ellie put on a bright smile, determined to be happy with this news.

"That's wonderful," Odelia said in a subdued manner.

Asher made a face. "I should have told Kent first," Asher suddenly said. "He *is* my client."

"No worries, my boy," Kent's hearty voice said, preceding his appearance by a mere heartbeat. "And it's about time, I say."

"Grandpa," Ellie said, rushing to his side. "Think what this means. We can go home as soon as the repairs are complete."

"I'll call the contractor," he said, smiling down at her. His gaze went then to Odelia. "But I have no intention of leaving this house. Ever. Unless my darling Odelia herself throws me out."

"Oh!" Odelia squeaked, her hands going to her cheeks. The next instant she launched herself forward, neatly avoiding the table and armchair as she ran toward him with outstretched arms. She'd produced a hanky from somewhere and waved it wildly. "Kent, do you mean it?"

He caught her hands in his. "I was foolish enough to try to take you from your sisters once before, my love. I'll do anything I must to never lose you again. I've just been waiting for this, so there would be no confusion as to my motives." He went down on one knee, to the gasps of several in the room—everyone, perhaps, except Asher. "Odelia, my heart, will you, at long last, make me the happiest of men and marry me?"

Hypatia staggered backward, while Magnolia plopped down on the settee behind her. Odelia hurled herself into Kent's arms.

"Yes! Yes! Yes! Yes!" she cried between pecking kisses that left vivid pink imprints on Kent's beaming face.

Delighted, Ellie clapped her hands and laughed. A grinning Asher stepped over and helped the happy couple rise, one hand clamped firmly under each of their arms.

"I don't believe it!" Hypatia breathed. "*You two* are the romance?"

"And what's wrong with that?" Odelia demanded, edging closer to Kent, who looped an arm protectively about her shoulders.

Magnolia cleared her throat and got to her feet once more. "Odelia, are you sure about this?"

"I'm going to marry Kent," Odelia insisted firmly, "and if you don't want us here, we will move to Charter Street." She lifted her chin, which Ellie noted was trembling.

"Of course we want you here," Hypatia said in a mollifying, slightly exasperated tone. "We're just…stunned by this…unexpected event."

"Unexpected?" Odelia echoed, snapping her hanky as if it were a whip. "It's been coming for fifty years!"

"So it has," Kent chuckled. "No rash actions for us, eh, my darling?"

Odelia cooed at him as if he'd just uttered the most clever, romantic words in history. Ellie blinked back tears at a dream realized.

Hypatia glanced pointedly at Magnolia, swallowed, tilted her head regally and said, "Quite right. Welcome to the f-family, Kent."

He made a courtly bow. "Thank you, dear sister, from the bottom of my heart."

Asher moved to Ellie's side and slipped an arm about her waist, smiling down at her as the chatter around them rose in volume. Magnolia demanded details of Odelia and Kent's "clandestine" romance, and they happily told the tale. Ellie dashed away tears, so very happy for her grandfather. Gazing up at Asher, she mouthed the words, *Thank you.*

He shook his head, asking softly, "For what?"

She went up on tiptoe to whisper in his ear, "For not advising her against him."

"I am going to recommend a prenup," Asher muttered.

Ellie just smiled at him. "I'm on to you, Asher Chatam. You're as much of a sappy romantic as the rest of us."

"You think so?"

"I do."

"We'll see."

"I suppose you'll want a proper wedding," Hypatia was saying.

"Oh, yes!" Odelia exclaimed before glancing up at Kent. "That is, we haven't discussed it."

"Whatever you want, my love," he told her, "but first things first, I always say. We haven't even purchased an engagement ring yet. I thought you'd like to choose your own this time."

Odelia squealed and clapped her hands around her hanky, while Hypatia muttered something about "gaudy bits" and Magnolia bit her lip.

"We'll be needing flowers," she said, launching to her feet and bustling toward the door. "*Lots* of flowers."

Hypatia turned and sat down heavily in her customary chair. Ellie almost felt sorry for her. Major change had finally come to Chatam House. For her grandfather and Odelia, Ellie couldn't have been happier, but the sisters had some huge adjustments in store.

She couldn't quite believe that her grandfather hadn't shared his feelings and details of the growing romance with her before this. Oh, she'd had clues, of course, but she had assumed that the older couple were taking it slowly. It had even occurred to her that they might have achieved all they really wanted, relationship-wise. At their ages, a deep friendship might have seemed as important as romance. It had never occurred to her that her grandfather might be waiting to pop the question until the matter of the insurance settlement was resolved.

"We have to go," Asher said, urging her toward the doorway. Ellie nodded somewhat reluctantly and moved with him in that direction.

It was a measure of Hypatia's distraction that she did not even note their departure. Odelia and Kent happily waved them on their way with wishes for a successful outcome to the game and went back to celebrating their engagement. Chuckling, Asher hurried Ellie out of the house and into his car.

On the drive to Dallas, Asher admitted to having known for some time that Kent intended to propose and had surmised that the old boy was just waiting for the insurance company to settle before doing so. He just hadn't expected a proposal on the spot. Ellie detailed her own suspicions about a burgeoning romance but confessed that she was taken off guard by this evening's events.

"Well, at any rate, you and Dallas have gotten your way," he told her. "I may even have to admit to her that she was right about the two of them all along."

"Oh, the horrors!" Ellie teased.

He laughed, guiding the vehicle off the highway, and she reflected silently how relaxed and pleased he seemed. Might he one day realize that she had played a part in that and hope to secure such for his future? On the other hand, why should he? Perhaps this was all he ever wanted, someone with whom to laugh and tease and spend time. Their kisses, while sweet, had certainly been few and far between.

She thought of her grandfather and Odelia and could not squelch a pang of envy.

Forgive me, Lord, she thought, as Ash drove through the busy streets of University Park. *Grandpa deserves his happiness, and it's been a long time coming. Thank You for answering my prayers on his behalf.*

Psalm 21:2 rolled through her mind. *You have granted him the desire of his heart and have not withheld the request of his lips.*

That followed the verse in the previous chapter that she had been praying for so long. Suddenly she felt compelled to pray that verse for herself, paraphrasing as needed.

May You give me the desire of my heart and make all my plans succeed.

It seemed selfish to pray on her own behalf in that manner, but hadn't Jabez asked for what he wanted? Hadn't David and Solomon and even Christ?

Not my will, Lord, but Yours. You know best. You always know best.

They reached the lighted soccer field. A small stadium, really, it boasted elevated seats and a concession stand offering peanuts, popcorn, nachos and pizza, along with sodas and water.

The team had already assembled. The team

manager had already unloaded the equipment and started warm-ups, but Asher did not go to the bench. Instead, he walked Ellie to the stands and suggested that she take a vacant space next to his sister on the third row up.

"Dallas!" she exclaimed, surprised. "I didn't know you were going to be here. Why didn't you ride with us?"

Her friend just shrugged and patted the metal bench next to her. As Ellie climbed over the bottom two rows, she noticed more familiar faces.

"Ilene. Angie. Shawna. What are you guys doing here?"

"It's a learning experience," Ilene told her. "We figured the kids could learn a thing or two by watching an older, select team."

"Good idea! Don't know why I didn't think of it myself." A glance around before she took her seat showed her other parents and kids from her team. Apparently, when Ilene said "we," she really meant "we."

"You won't believe what's happened," she said to Dallas, as she made herself comfortable on the bench. "Odelia and Kent are engaged!"

Dallas grabbed her hand, squealed and stomped her feet. "That's fabulous! That's fabulous! I knew it would work. I knew it!" Hopping up, she cupped her hands around her mouth and bawled at her brother, "I told you so!"

To the laughter of those around them, Asher turned, shrugged and lifted both arms in a gesture of acceptance. Dallas dropped back down and begged for details, which Ellie eagerly furnished. As they chortled over Asher's having to help the happy couple to their feet after Kent's dramatic proposal, the ref trotted to the center of the field and blew his whistle to start the game.

It was an exciting match. Ellie couldn't resist the opportunity to instruct those of her players present, and she continually pointed out good moves and explained strategies. With four minutes left to play, Asher's team was down by a single goal.

"Still time, still time," Ellie chanted, twisting her hands together.

With two minutes left, she started rooting for a tie and overtime. But the other team's defense just proved too strong. Ash's goalie hung his head as he made his way to the sideline, but Asher went out to meet him and brought him in with an arm looped about his shoulders.

As the team huddled up, people started leaving the stands, but when Ellie rose, Dallas yanked her right back down again.

"Ow!"

"Just hang on," her friend counseled. "Give Ash a minute with his team."

Ellie sat again, noticing that they weren't the only ones staying put. Suddenly a whistle blew, and Asher's team jogged back onto the field. Confused, Ellie was just about to ask Dallas what was going on. Just then, the team split apart and ran in opposite directions, unrolling a banner between them.

"What on…"

Her words died away as the banner came into view. It read, "Ellie, will you marry me?" And there in front of the stands, Asher spread his arms wide, staring up at her with a question in his eyes.

For a long moment Ellie didn't move. She'd clapped a hand over her mouth and just sat there staring at him. Only when Dallas shoved her did she stumble to her feet and start climbing down to the field. As she did so, people began applauding. Asher didn't think she even heard. By the time her feet met the tarmac on the path in front of the stands, she was crying.

"Are you serious?" she squeaked at him.

In response, Asher dropped down onto one knee and reached into the pocket of his jacket for the ring box he'd stashed there. He tried to joke, saying, "Kent stole a bit of my thunder." With his heart in his throat, it came out sounding pretty strangled.

This had all seemed like such a good idea when he'd discussed it with Dallas earlier. He'd wanted to do something fun, something that his exuberant Ellie would love. But maybe she didn't love him after all. Maybe he'd rushed her. Maybe he'd been so sensible and so stoic for so long that he just couldn't pull off something this wild.

She stood there with her hands over her mouth, and he started to feel like a fool. What now? Get up and walk away? Try to live the rest of his life without her? He couldn't even imagine such a thing. Not now.

Clearing his throat, he tried to remember all the eloquent words he'd practiced, but they came only sluggishly to his mind. "You were right. I had let failure mark me, and I wouldn't let God take it away. Instead, I clung to it, used it like a shield against any possibility of…romance." There. He'd said it. Silly word, *romance*. Silly, essential, wonderful word. "Then you came. I think I should more rightly say that God sent you. I've learned so much from you, Ellie. Mostly, I think, I've learned to love."

"Ash."

"I love you, Ellie. I love you."

Apparently, he got it all right because she dropped her hands, sniffed and said, "I love you, too!"

He breathed a tiny sigh of relief and got to his feet at last. "Without even knowing it, I've been waiting for you, waiting for you to grow up. Waiting for God to bring us together." She stood there staring at him with the world in her watery, violet eyes and a smile on her ruby lips, and he couldn't resist a quip. "Waiting for you to say yes."

She burst out laughing. "Yes!"

"Whew!" He started to open the ring box, but suddenly she threw herself at him, her arms encircling his neck. Laughing, he swung her around in a circle to the applause and laughter of their secretly invited audience.

When he sat her on her feet again, she gazed up at him with love in her eyes and exclaimed, "I can't believe you're serious!"

"Sweetheart," he said, keeping a straight face. "I'm always serious. Everyone knows that."

They laughed again, and he finally got that little box open and the ring on her finger. Every woman within shouting distance ran to see the rock he'd picked out. By the way she kept looking at it and him, he knew he'd chosen well.

Asher shook his head at the wonder of it all as his back was clapped and congratulations rang in his ears. He'd once thought himself too busy for love, but now he realized that he'd kept busy because his life was so empty that he'd had to fill it up. Now that God had brought the right woman to him, his life and his heart were full to overflowing.

Who would have guessed that it would be Ellie, though? Young, exuberant, absolutely perfect Ellie.

When the crowd dwindled to a select few, Asher couldn't wait any longer to pull her into his arms and kiss her. He lifted his head a few moments later, happiness swelling his heart, and noticed Dallas standing nearby in tears. He hadn't expected that from his headstrong little sister, but she was the unrepentant romantic. She surprised him again when she said, "I'm sorry your team lost." As if that mattered!

"Did they?" he quipped. "Hadn't noticed. Must've had something else on my mind." Ellie giggled and slid her arms around his waist.

Suddenly, Dallas's face crumpled and noisy sobs grated out of her. Ellie slipped out of his arms to go to her.

"Dallas?"

"I have to tell you something," she gasped, holding up a hand as if to hold off Ellie's comfort. "I did it. The fire. It was my fault."

"What?" Asher blurted, stunned.

She turned her tear-filled eyes on Ellie. "You told me you were going to be at the storage unit, right after you told me how awful the fumes were in the house, and that if they didn't get better you might have to move out for a few days." She gulped and went on. "I was going to go by while you were gone and make sure all the windows were closed so the fumes wouldn't dissipate, then wait for you to come in and suggest that you stay at Chatam House for a couple of days."

When she'd found that the door was open, however, she'd gone in, and on her way to check the window, she'd turned on the lamp. That was when she'd seen the bucket with the can of paint remover and come up with the idea of removing the cap, but she'd dropped the can and spilled the liquid. The fumes had been so awful that she'd opened the window after finding it already closed. The cat had jumped into the room, and when she'd chased him, he'd jumped up onto the table and knocked over the lamp.

"There was nothing I could do!" she wailed in a small voice. "I ran out the front door in a panic and into the street. Garrett nearly ran me over on his motorcycle. The rest you know."

Asher stood there dumbfounded while Ellie sighed. "I knew I'd shut that window."

The truth hit Asher like a ton of bricks. "And

you knew that she shouldn't have been at the house. You were protecting her!"

Ellie grimaced and nodded. "In the end, I did try to tell you."

"And I all but accused you of setting the fire."

"You didn't accuse me. You rightly suspected that I hadn't told you everything." She looked at Dallas. "Just as I suspected that Dallas had had something to do with it."

"I'm so sorry, Ellie!" Dallas exclaimed. "I should've told you right away, but then you'd have known I was scheming, and I didn't want you to think badly of me."

Ellie turned an agonized look on Asher. "The insurance company."

"We have to tell them," he said quietly, "but I don't think it will make any difference. Ultimately, it was all an accident."

"Now I have to say something," Ellie told him, stepping close again. "You suspected that my grandfather and I were involved with the fire, and I took great offense at that, but all the time I was guilty of the same thing with Dallas." She looked at her friend and admitted, "I actually thought you might have done it on purpose."

Dallas parked her hands at her waist and threw out one hip. "Well, thank you very much."

"It wasn't that unreasonable of an assumption,"

Asher told her. She rolled her eyes, but her teeth worried her bottom lip.

"You're sure this isn't going to set back things with the insurance company?"

"Don't worry about it," he said. "I'll take care of everything."

She laughed, that incorrigible redhead, and wiped her eyes. "Don't you always? Boy, that's a load off my shoulders."

Ellie turned her gaze up at him then. "You do, you know, always take care of everything. That's why you wouldn't let up about the fire. You knew I'd held back information."

"And I was afraid for you," he admitted softly.

She brushed a hand across his chest. "I want you to know that I wasn't angry so much as I was hurt that day," she said. "I was hurt because I so desperately wanted you to care about me."

"I care," he said, wrapping his arms around her. "I cared then. I was just so bound up in the armor I'd created to make myself impervious to love that I couldn't admit it, even to myself. But you'd already worked your way into my heart. I think you've been there all along. I couldn't let you go." He pulled her closer. "I won't let you go."

Squaring her slender shoulders, Dallas exclaimed, "Wow! I'm even better than I thought I was at this matchmaking thing."

His sister the matchmaker. Asher shuddered at

the thought, but then he looked down at Ellie and smiled. Maybe she did have a kind of instinct for the job.

"Just think," Dallas went on. "The aunties have two weddings to plan now!"

"Let them have at it," he said, gazing down at his Ellie. "So long as they do it quickly," he amended.

Laughing, she lifted up on tiptoe and pressed her lips to his.

Odelia and Kent might have had fifty years to fool around, he thought, but he was a busy man, a man in a hurry to claim all the joy that God allowed.

* * * * *

Dear Reader,

You've surely met those with whom you seem to have "everything" in common. Conversely, you must've met those to whom you could barely relate. Background, age, ethnicity, language, social status, politics, religion...so many things can come between us. Often, however, if we give ourselves an opportunity to get to know someone with whom we seemingly have little in common, we find that a very special relationship forms.

Such is the case with a young lady who wrote me from her native Zimbabwe as a twelve-year-old. After years of correspondence, we were able to meet in person. I still marvel that a girl born and raised in another culture on another continent could come to occupy such a large place in my heart! I pray that you will give yourself a chance, like Asher and Ellie, to know such "unlikely" joy.

God bless,

Arlene James

QUESTIONS FOR DISCUSSION

1. Asher Chatam is a man who sincerely tries to do what is right. He lives by a strong ethical standard—one does not date a client; a man must not be attracted to his baby sister's best friend; and so on. Why don't others (for instance, his cousin Chandler and the aunties) feel as strongly about his convictions as he does?

2. Asher believed himself to be unsuitable for marriage. Do you know individuals who are clearly meant to remain unmarried? Is it possible, then, that some—even those not involved in "church" occupations—are *called* to singlehood? Explain.

3. Have you ever been tempted, like Ellie and Dallas, to "assist" God in working out His will? Is this a good idea? Why or why not?

4. Dallas schemed to get Odelia and Kent together. Ellie reasoned that she was merely "facilitating" that romance. Is "facilitating" different from "scheming" in this case? Explain.

5. Psalm 20:4 reads, "May He give you the desire of your heart and make all your plans

succeed." Ellie prayed this prayer on behalf of her grandfather. Have you ever prayed this prayer on behalf of another individual? If so, why?

6. Psalm 21:2 reads, "You have granted him the desire of his heart and have not withheld the request of his lips." This verse appears to show that God answered the prayer of the psalmist in the previous chapter. If you have prayed a prayer similar to Psalm 20:4 (see above), what happened?

7. How do you define *romance?*

8. Asher felt that romance created problems and interfered with life. He just didn't have time for it. Is this premise valid in any way? If so, how?

9. Is romance necessary for marriage? Is it desirable for marriage?

10. Odelia feared that she and Kent were too old for romance. Asher agreed. Ellie did not. What is your opinion?

11. Ideally, marriage is a partnership in which two people join forces and build a life together. This often includes acquiring a home

and possessions, having children, making mutual friends, setting and achieving mutual goals. Why, then, do you think *older* individuals marry?

12. Does age "matter" when it comes to marriage? Explain.

13. In your opinion, should older (elderly) couples marry? Why or why not?

14. Asher is fifteen years older than Ellie. He felt this would be a problem; she did not. What is an acceptable age difference for marriage partners and why?

15. Ellie and Asher have two major commonalities. They are both Christians, and they both enjoy soccer. How important do you think this is? Can you identify other commonalities?

LARGER-PRINT BOOKS!

GET 2 FREE
LARGER-PRINT NOVELS
PLUS 2 FREE
MYSTERY GIFTS

Love Inspired®

Larger-print novels are now available...

YES! Please send me 2 FREE LARGER-PRINT Love Inspired® novels and my 2 FREE mystery gifts (gifts are worth about $10). After receiving them, if I don't wish to receive any more books, I can return the shipping statement marked "cancel". If I don't cancel, I will receive 6 brand-new novels every month and be billed just $4.74 per book in the U.S. or $5.24 per book in Canada. That's a saving of at least 24% off the cover price. It's quite a bargain! Shipping and handling is just 50¢ per book in the U.S. and 75¢ per book in Canada.* I understand that accepting the 2 free books and gifts places me under no obligation to buy anything. I can always return a shipment and cancel at any time. Even if I never buy another book, the two free books and gifts are mine to keep forever.

122/322 IDN FC79

Name	(PLEASE PRINT)

Address		Apt. #

City	State/Prov.	Zip/Postal Code

Signature (if under 18, a parent or guardian must sign)

Mail to the **Reader Service:**
IN U.S.A.: P.O. Box 1867, Buffalo, NY 14240-1867
IN CANADA: P.O. Box 609, Fort Erie, Ontario L2A 5X3

Not valid to current subscribers to Love Inspired Larger-Print books.

**Are you a current subscriber to Love Inspired books
and want to receive the larger-print edition?
Call 1-800-873-8635 or visit www.ReaderService.com.**

* Terms and prices subject to change without notice. Prices do not include applicable taxes. Sales tax applicable in N.Y. Canadian residents will be charged applicable taxes. Offer not valid in Quebec. This offer is limited to one order per household. All orders subject to credit approval. Credit or debit balances in a customer's account(s) may be offset by any other outstanding balance owed by or to the customer. Please allow 4 to 6 weeks for delivery. Offer available while quantities last.

Your Privacy—The Reader Service is committed to protecting your privacy. Our Privacy Policy is available online at www.ReaderService.com or upon request from the Reader Service.

We make a portion of our mailing list available to reputable third parties that offer products we believe may interest you. If you prefer that we not exchange your name with third parties, or if you wish to clarify or modify your communication preferences, please visit us at www.ReaderService.com/consumerchoice or write to us at Reader Service Preference Service, P.O. Box 9062, Buffalo, NY 14269. Include your complete name and address.